T0116256
Howl of the Ocean

These scribblings are dedicated to my wife, Caroline.

(Actually, my wife doesn't read fantasy,
so perhaps someone could tell her
otherwise she'll never know!)

My contribution to your bathroom library, for peace, plop and posterity!
Cover painting of Gam by Eva Widermann. Logo by Lydia Schuchmann.
Be sure to visit www.paulbillinghurst.com for merry little snippets and tinkerings

Order this book online at www.trafford.com
or email orders@trafford.com

Most Trafford titles are also available at major online book retailers.

Note for Librarians: A cataloguing record for this book is available from Library and Archives Canada at www.collectionscanada.ca/amicus/index-e.html

Printed in Victoria, BC, Canada.

ISBN: 978-1-4120-5566-6 (sc)
ISBN: 978-1-4269-1479-9 (hc)

Our mission is to efficiently provide the world's finest, most comprehensive book publishing service, enabling every author to experience success. To find out how to publish your book, your way, and have it available worldwide, visit us online at www.trafford.com

Trafford rev. 09/24/09

www.trafford.com

North America & international
toll-free: 1 888 232 4444 (USA & Canada)
phone: 250 383 6864 • fax: 812 355 4082

A rocky outcrop juts into the rough ocean fray like a spearhead. Here the wind churns the sea, creating whirlpools like some portal to the Abyss. The men of Barrowdale refer to the point as the Howl of the Ocean; the bravest of pirates that sail the coastal point call the area *Dead Man's Scream*. Few can explain the eerie shriek that emanates from this small area of secluded and wind-swept coast. Some say it is the ocean, screaming its warnings of the end of the world. Others say that it is haunted by the restless spirits of long, hung pirates - known as Sea Spectres. Whatever folklore sprouted its name, a small settlement known as Frostcross has formed in the crook of two hills adjacent to the rocky outcrop. Overlooking this frontier town of cutthroats, stands a small, stone chapel but its tolling bell is no match against the...

PROLOGUE

13th Noon, Lunar Cycle of Mondeth's Star, 1189 Winters.

The mountain ridge of Montasp, a jagged wall of stone and ice rising out of the mists. This rocky wall ended suddenly at the brink of a murky nothingness and from somewhere far below came the dull roar of an unseen waterfall and fast rolling river, a river that ran into the Dead Maw – a body of water that marked the boundary of Cheth Chandor.

The frothy waters filled the air with a fine mist that near froze and turned to a light snow. To the side of the ridge and the ongoing spires of Montasp's lofty peaks - gaining ice and snow as they disappeared into the clouds - stood the small city of Cheth Chandor, situated on a lower plato overlooking the valleys that eventually led to Barrowdale.

The city nestled next to a vast rock wall of the ever-rising mountain range, as if protecting itself from the worst of the elements, especially today as the snow was falling thick and fast.

A rowdy congregation of Chandorian citizens, wrapped tightly in many layers of furs and leathers, hurried in the thick snow as best as they could, as not even the accursed winter season weather would stop them from witnessing justice served against the infamous pirate king known as the Wraith. Justice in the form of a thick, rope noose.

With piercing eyes, comparable by folk to that of the devil's, he studied the Executioner as the masked man uttered his worthless words of mercy. The Wraith did not yearn for such drivel, he was condemned but openly culpable and as he awaited his fate - the fate that came with the click and release of the trap door below his heavy-set feet - he just couldn't give a damn.

He was called the Wraith for the shock of long white hair that cascaded down behind him, now though it was shawn close to his head to prevent mites in the terrible squalor of the cell that had been his home for the last twelve days. He also sported a dozen days worth of stubble and white facial hair. He was tall, lean and strong, made that way by a tough life at sea and leading by violent example. He was left dressed in the tattered remains of his once ornately buckled seaman's cloak. The black, light leather armour he usually wore had been stripped from him together with a wide baldric that had housed his stiletto throwing blades and basket hilted sabre that was his lethal companion for so many terror campaigns. In more recent times he had even adopted a beaten-metal mask in the form of a ghostly visage to enhance his feared reputation as the Wraith - self-professed pirate king of Hauntmouth Point.

Now, stripped of all his frightening finery he looked almost ordinary. It was that which made him so feared, he was normal to the eye but behind that calm visage he was cold, cunning and calculating, well versed in the manipulation of others and he took great pleasure from things that very few could even stomach. His reputation ran to an unhealthy addiction in practicing demonology and tap-room whispers even revealed a vile hunger for necrophilia.

The Wraith breathed in the crisp air but all he could taste was death. The rain cooled his brow, his torn cloak dancing with the wind. His limbs went numb, his mind emptied and he was resolved to his fate. The savagery, the butchery of a life such as his would afford no God to sway the hand of justice. He remembered the screams, the whimpers, night after night. He couldn't recall a single face now, too many was his count - the rampant murders, the faceless and the phantom - raped and butchered, his want for gold and pleasure in torment was absolute.

The Executioner faulted and stopped as a smile played about the corner of the Wraith's lips and he announced to the throng in a strong voice, "slay me, take me, but never will you forget me. I have been your doom and I will come again fore my darkness is never ending and the light snuffs at my bidding, just like your weak tedious lives..." He eyed the lever that would send him to his death and the memory of his capture came to prominence - when he was so entrapped by that sickeningly smooth hero, and he couldn't help but cry out his name in hatred, "Raklen Mortlake I curse you from the pits of the Abyss, you're a dead man, I swear it!" He then turned to the Executioner and stared unflinching into his eyes and added, "and I am so bloody sick of you."

In silent reply the Chandorian Executioner turned away, whispering a prayer for his own benefit than the condemned.

The stunned crowd quietened with baited breath, the moan of the winter wind now prominent once again. All that could be discerned in between the gusts were the Executioner's droning voice and the occasional clink of a Chandorian Militiaman's chain mail. Still the Wraith smiled on in conceit.

Below the stage area stood a Militia Sergeant and the one who had been given the sterling command of the execution detachment, a task that he had grudgingly accepted. He had witnessed more hellish hangings than he could count but it was this one in particular that had generated so much interest and anxiety and had drawn the largest crowd that he could remember. He was a lean man, but over recent winters too much Barrowdale brew had given him a paunch that bulged under his padded leather and chain mail armour. If he didn't ease up soon - as his wife often preached - there would soon be no sign of that once lean frame.

He pushed the face of his spitting wife from his mind and focused on the two figures on the platform above him. He could just make out the Wraith mouthing off at Wilten, the Executioner, after the Pirate's outburst at young Mortlake but the only word he actually discerned was *sick*.

The Sergeant gripped his halberd tightly and scanned the crowd, he indicated to his men to do the same. The silence was now palpable.

Wilten reached and heaved on the trapdoor handle but the click that signaled the release of the platform beneath the Pirate's feet never came. The Executioner stared at the handle for a brief moment then tried it again. Nothing.

What came next was sudden and shocking and the Sergeant was only able to gawp and watch as the vile scene played out in front of him just like his infrequent trips to the theatre. A dagger appeared - sailing through the air - and landed at the Wraith's feet. The self-professed pirate king dropped to retrieve it as Wilten urgently proceeded to strike the lever with his booted foot to get it working. At the same time a large rabble of citizen's unfurled their city garb to reveal themselves as pirates and charge the Chandorian militia.

As the Sergeant shook himself into action he parried a cutlass striking for his head and dared a quick glance to the platform, he realised it was a fatal error to take his eyes off his foe but he had to understand what was happening. The Wraith, a veteran in his own right, had retrieved the dagger and though still bound had managed to plunge it brutally into Wilten's neck. He must have hit the major artery as an inordinate amount of blood gushed into the air. The Sergeant was momentarily blinded as blood struck his face but in doing so his subsequent jerk-reaction allowed him to inadvertently dodge another cutlass strike.

The crowd started to scream as panic rippled through the throng like a chilling wave and the citizens of Cheth Chandor began to flee for their lives, trampling those unfortunate enough to get knocked down in the rush.

The Sergeant urgently wiped the blood from his face and shouted orders to his men. He grabbed a startled soldier and pushed him at his own assailant allowing him to disengage the combat and attempt to tackle the Wraith, who by this time had cut his noose and bonds and was already crossing the platform.

The Sergeant shoved away a citizen who was in his way, as he hastily made his way around the platform to engage the Wraith on the other side, when a prickling sensation to the back of his neck made him turn just in time to fend off two cursing pirates that had hurled themselves - with no concern to their own safety - at the Sergeant. The first was skewered by the soldier who was covering his Sergeant's withdrawal, sacrificing himself, but the other hollered with success as he got through to the Sergeant. It was a bold, if suicidal move and revealed how fanatical these brigands were to their pirate Captain. The crazed assailant spat oaths as the Sergeant hurried to block the pirate's wild swings and realised; looking into his attacker's rolling eyes, that he appeared drugged. No wonder their care for self-preservation was non-existent.

Fending off his attacker, the Sergeant took in the platform with his peripheral vision and noted what was simply a dark shadow leap from the stage and disappear into the crowd. As the Sergeant went to call out to any Militia that might be nearby and unengaged, he noted two things. One was a figure on horseback who appeared to be overseeing the commotion from a high plato and raising it's arms, the second, was a series of eruptions around the platform that sent Chandorian Militiamen and pirates alike reeling into the air. Blood and limbs rained down around the Sergeant as he was knocked from his feet by the erupting timber platform and a heavy section of hurtling oak beam caved his head in and everything went black.

The small, cloaked figure on the overlooking outcrop relaxed in satisfaction and gathered up the reigns of the horse to move off. A figure with curves not befitting a man and sitting in a saddle marked with a haunting, spectral face – the icon of the Wraith.

***

13th Eve, Lunar Cycle of Mondeth's Star, 1189 Winters.

Castle Mortlake sat prominently on a high rocky shelf of Montasp overlooking the winding and affluent district of Cheth Chandor. The castle was large and constructed of strong granite mined from the surrounding Montasp Mountain Range and its near impregnable walls sat proudly adjacent to a large body of water, ebony in hue, and where the fortification and noble family therein had originally gained their proud name.

The wind was strong and high above the castle's courtyard, several flags attached to the Keep flapped vigorously and noisily. A small contingent of the Mortlake Guard shuffled nervously, gripping long spears but kept a respectful distance from two men, stern of stature, whom stood stoic and still at the entrance to the Mortlake chapel. The first and older man stood slightly forward, a veteran soldier judging by his strong bearing and sporting a long trailing moustache that only leaders of men could carry off. His regal black surcoat displayed the Mortlake crest consisting of a Keep above a lake and indicated his position as head of the family. With hands on hips he surveyed a gruesome scene in front of him and indicated to the armoured captain of the guard standing at his shoulder.

"Send a warning to my son." The old Mortlake proclaimed stepping to the side and allowing the captain to view the family's Chaplain nailed to the door of the chapel, a note snagged on a large iron nail hammered through his chest. Over the captain's gasps the head of the Mortlake family continued, "It is more than simply a note of revenge against my son. The Wraith is telling us he can get to anyone he wants and will go to any lengths..."

CHAPTER ONE

26th Night, Lunar Cycle of the Cursed Constellation, 1189 Winters.

The Fool's Nook tavern sign swung in the prevailing wind, creaking a rhythm as steady as a heartbeat. The rhythmic groan faltered as a heavy gust caught the sign hanging in front of the murky frontage of the spit and sawdust drinking establishment and blew it off one of its hinges. The gentle creaking was now replaced by a piercing screech as the rusting bracket protested against the unbalanced weight. As a countenance to the cacophony, the tavern's door thundered open, shedding a tall square of lamp light out onto the slick cobbles of the lane. A chorus of shouts, curses and laughter momentarily drowned out the noise from above, until the door closed, leaving Braggers Lane dark once again.

A new noise was now introduced to the rain-slick lane; ragged breathing of a man well past his prime, like age-old salted beef. Dragon's breath fogged the air as the man gasped and hobbled far quicker than his old legs would normally allow and followed a steady stream of mutterings as he slipped on the wet cobbles. A light rain began to swirl in the wind and an eerie illumination swept over the craggy landscape as the moon won over the heavy-laden clouds.

The old man glanced up, at last being able to pick over the uneven ground with greater ease and quickened his ungainly pace. The water drizzled onto his balding head and soaked his matted long hair, running down wrinkled and leathery skin in rivulets, taking the water around his staring eyes. Eyes, which after closer, horrifying inspection, were not merely staring but were unnaturally formed that way - for the old man's eyelids were missing.

Jonah the Lidless was his name, an old sea dog and Barrowdale citizen that was always seen frequenting Frostcross's dog-hole centre – the Fool's Nook Inn. Often he was seen wandering the coastal paths around Frostcross and Barrowdale staring longingly out to the brimy surf. Children often teased that Jonah was as old as the ocean, a father of pirates, simply because he looked the part. The old man always kept to himself mostly because of his hideous deformity. It was said that as punishment for falling asleep whilst on lookout in the Crow's Nest at the top of the ship's mast, his torturous captain cut away his eyelids so that he would never do so again. Whatever the truth of Jonah's background, tonight – a typical late eve of the early season – he was running scared, like a man just keeping ahead of the Reaper's scythe.

"Between the demon and the deep sea!" Cursed Jonah, stumbling again as he at last cleared the boundary of Frostcross and headed down the well-worn Shoremeet lane towards the coast. He cast another terrified glance behind him as his fist closed tighter around a small, browning parchment sticking out between his fingers. He held it close and reverently to his chest as if it were an internal organ and his life depended on it. He glanced left and then right as an owl hooted somewhere off to his right and he jumped, dropping his ornately carved walking stick and supported himself against a lone, spindly tree. He pushed himself away from it in haste and in doing so gaining a quicker, scuttling pace.

The wind picked up, whipping the rain into his face, causing his eyes to sting and shed tears with no eyelids to protect them. He raised his arms to shield his face, clutching the parchment still in favour of reclaiming his walking aid.

A sudden snap of a breaking twig came echoing to his ears and spurred him on even more. The wind blew his cloak and it snagged and held on a tree, its branches reaching down to the lane, leafless and old like gnarled hands trying to snag him. He pulled on the cloak, it momentarily held, pinning him and then with one final heave, it ripped and came free catching him off guard. The sudden freedom caused him to fall, sending him painfully down to his elderly knees. He risked a quick glance behind again and thought he saw something glinting in the moon's casting light. Somehow, even with old muscles aching he willed himself up and fled further down the lane.

His breathing became even more ragged and seared his lungs as he pushed on, no further noise came from behind and he dared to let himself think he had lost his pursuer - but only for a brief moment. In his state? Who was he kidding? Many winters had passed since he had been able to even outrun a creeping vine.

As he negotiated a particularly rough area of ground that marked the edge of a fast-flowing brook and foot bridge, his mind raced - unlike his passage across the bridge - to that face he had witnessed staring at him across the Fool's Nook Inn - a face that was now burned into his mind, one that he had not seen in several winters and one that he would wish never to set eyes on again. The shock had sent him fleeing out into the night and now on this lonely lane, possibly even his death.

Jonah limped across the timbers of the footbridge, the resounding thud of his footfalls rivalling the thudding pulse in his head. He reached the far bank, this time not daring to glance back in case his fears became too fearfully true and his pursuer was gaining on him. His cabin came into view on the crest of the hill; he could just make it out through his stinging vision. Relief flooded over him and in his haste he slipped on an area of moss-covered stones, going down hard. He cracked his knee on a jagged rock and a howl of pain escaped from his lips. He grasped his knee with his parchment-clenched hand and reached out with his other, blindly feeling for an outcropping stone or nook in which he could haul himself along with, gaining at least small precious distance until the pain subsided enough for him to stand.

The rain hammered down upon his back, the coldness numbing his extremities but also probably stopping him from falling unconscious. His old body just couldn't take this kind of strain anymore. He focused on getting himself up, the owl hooted again and it allowed him to come to his senses – to focus, to beat the pain and not let the coldness take hold of him in its deathly grip. His bony, reaching fingers found a slimy timber and urgently snatched at it, his finger nails digging into the wet wood and with some new found inner strength - focusing on the safety of the cabin just beyond this next meadow - he heaved himself up onto the stile.

A loud whistle cut through the rain. Jonah never saw the missiles flight but he heard its impact a heartbeat before he felt it. The arrowhead and shaft were just visible through the ancient Mariner's chest – he stared down at it in disbelief and an eternity seemed to pass. He went to grab at it but the pain exploding from his chest made him falter and slip from the stile and he came crashing down on the other side. His face slapped into the muddy ground, jarring his body and snapping the vicious barbed arrow sprouting from his chest. The pain was unbearable and he clawed at the ground in desperation, the terror of the pursuit still lodged in his mind. He somehow clawed and crawled his way to an old twisted and knobbly tree and summoning all his last waning strength lifted his arm and thrust the parchment into the crook of two low boughs. He pushed himself immediately away from the time-gnarled trunk – feverish whisperings of some limbless statue escaping from dry, cracked lips. Jonah continued to claw at the ground, the earth cutting under his fingernails as he heaved himself along.

A second whistle split the air and Jonah found himself counting his racing pulse. He counted three before he cried out with pain and the impact of the second arrow drove him hard into the muddy ground.

Light footsteps made their way around the prone body. The arrow shaft was reclaimed. Quick hands searched through the clothes and then, as the wind died too, a blood spattered leaf came to rest upon the cooling corpse, eyes still staring.

At last Jonah slept in darkness.

***

The morning wind howled down the grassy undulating hills, pushing the trees and gorse bushes into a constant pitch. The wind whistled through a copse of trees on the hills face, causing the birds nesting in their lofty boughs to caw. It buffeted grazing sheep standing in their grassy troughs and sent a family of rabbits hopping through primroses and snowdrops to the safety of their cosy burrow.

The wind raced back up the meadow valley to the summit of the next hill overlooking the settlement of Frostcross and blew through the small opening atop the vine-wrapped, stone tower of a small Chapel - no larger than for twenty or so worshippers - and causing its bell to toll one deep resonating tone. The wind wailed through the ancient moss-clad headstones and grass reclaiming tombs scattered over the small hillside – only the occasional yawning opening signifying that a small tomb was even there. The gale trilled down the hill and Bragger Lane, battering the hedgerow and tussled the fur on the backend of a reclusive badger that soon completely disappeared from sight. The strong gust channelled down the lane and continued through the small settlement of ramshackle and stone buildings until it caught the already half-hanging sign of the Fool's Nook Inn and blew it completely off its last hinge, sending it crashing down to the cobbles below.

"Look out!" shouted the Innkeeper appearing from the cellar trapdoor, more to himself than anyone else. His grimy apron was swept up in the gale and flapped momentarily over his face, "High-Hag's-spore!" He cursed, clicking his tongue. He pushed down his leather apron, eyeing the broken sign now rocking gently on the ground and shook his head, wearily closing the trapdoor and sliding the heavy bolt back into place. He did this instinctively however, as he was solely concentrating on how much hard-earned coin he would have to impart with in order to fix the sign. If it were possible, he was even grumpier now.

He wiped his hand backward through his shoulder-length, unkempt and grey hair and stopped to watch the dancing, dead leaves swirl across the lane until the wind dispersed. The old Inn-keeper mumbled something half discernible about why on Grand-pappy's-beard was he stopping to watch the be-damned-dancing-leaves! He hadn't the time for that and quickly turned - ever grumbling - straight into the path of some cloak-wrapped, tricorn-wearing stranger, causing him to jump and mutter - not apologise - oaths aplenty like a grudge-bearing, long-in-the-tooth dwarf.

"Jumpy aren't we?" spoke the stranger, his face barely visible over the top of his high-collared cloak and snugly fitting tricorn. To the common Innkeep his voice was sickeningly smooth and silky and he held the Innkeeper's ratty gaze fixed in piercing, confident green eyes.

"Aye! And ye would be too if a be-damned sign nearly broke atop your 'ead!" replied the Innkeeper in a gruff manner. The stranger smiled with his eyes - his mouth still covered - and glanced down, drawing the Innkeeper's eyes down also.

"Yours?" he asked in equally a dulcet tone. He held a weathered walking stick carved from Ash, which ended in a handle carved into the form of a busty maiden, not dissimilar to a ship's figurehead.

"Nay! Not mine!" replied the Innkeeper in haste and a sudden fit of helpfulness; the urge to get back to the warmth and shelter of the Fool's Nook outweighing any other desire.

"Then who's?" asked the man, catching the Innkeeper's arm as he tried to push passed him to the door. Something about the gesture made the Innkeeper rapidly halt, either the strength and determination of the grip or the penetrating coldness that made the old barman baulk with surprise and a sudden overwhelming feeling of co-operation.

"Old J..Jonah's," he mumbled. "Jonah!" He repeated louder and clearer when the stranger's grip increased, something about those piercing eyes just made him want to impart whatever information he could to get away from this devil of a man.

"He was 'ere yester eve makin' merry, went 'ome before the heavy rains set in he did, looked spooked like he saw some damn sea-spectre! He must 'ave dropped it I'd say. He lives yonder, cabin lookin' over the point – up that way," he finished, pointing.

"Did he have anyone with him?"

The Innkeeper paused in thought. The grip tightened again. "N..Nope, though someone did leave after 'im, now ye come to mention it, but I…"

The man silenced him by gently, yet threateningly, knocking the walking stick against the Innkeeper's chest, "and whom oversees the running of this little hovel of a settlement hmm?"

"No one really. Ardd, the old priest acted as a sort a lawman but e's been dead for near on two seasons now."

The green eyes looked away, sparkling knowingly and observed the lane running out of Frostcross. Not looking back to the Innkeeper he whispered, "I'll return this stick to its rightful owner then," and released his grip. "Now off with ye!"

Grateful to have finished the shortest, if most unsettling, conversation he had ever had, the Innkeeper rushed inside. However, curiosity in the unknown made him stop just inside, reopen the door but a jar and gaze after the creepy, silken-voiced stranger. He was already gone.

The old Innkeeper shuddered involuntarily and reassuringly rubbed the lucky seaman's tattoo on his forearm, "spirits be restless," he intoned watching the strong wind lift and sweep the inn sign across the lane in the stranger's wake. "Calling all manner of curses – folk and otherwise, down on us."

The wind sent the sign splintering into the side of a stone building at the point where he had lost sight of the stranger. Omen or not, the old Innkeeper shuddered again.

***

After a very hale and hearty - if befuddled - stroll, a very portly fellow found himself at a solid oak door of the small, humble chapel over-looking Frostcross and curiously, found it locked and sealed. His tanned, shiny face was framed by huge sideburns, which covered most of his cheeks, perhaps to compensate for the lack of hair above. An extra chin graced his neck, hanging over a stained, brown robe.

Gam – Warrior-priest, his second and quite new vocation. His first was best described as church Roofer and, in whispered tones, inebriated Friar. Hailing from Tinhallow Abbey, his very own sanctimonious brothers had convinced the Father Superior to send him to re-open the chapel of Frostcross, 'as, quite frankly,' they had smugly exclaimed, 'he just doesn't fit in!'

Gam shook his head remembering the incident and how the Father Superior had broken the news to him. Sure, he was an ale-swigging friar that wore the characteristically humble brown robes that were in fact so marked with ale-stains that one could no longer tell where the ale ended and the brown material began - but his reverent prayers were often answered.

Gam glanced up to the moss, lichen and other leafy debris crusting the roof slates and tutted, whistled and finally guffawed. He shook the hastily slung chains and locks criss-crossing the doors and then, with no more than a shrug of the shoulders and a short gripe that someone should have given him a key, he continued on his merry way, skirting tombs, skipping over stone markers and swaggering out of the decaying gateway.

After a short delay rescuing his foot from the portal of an under-construction bunny burrow - ignoring the curt look from the nearby furry fabricator - Gam began a pie-eyed stroll across the meadow toward Frostcross, an old favoured tune escaping his lips. An early liquid lunch was definitely on the cards.

"O the chalk-white cliffs by the sea, came a lady
dancing with glee,
her tresses were raven, and did bounce with her swayin',
as the animals danced at her feet.

Hey-ho, Honey, hey, over the hills she will play,
hey-ho, sings the honey bee, come fair maiden
and dance with me.

Flowers sprung with our steps in the meadow,
birds a spiralling to lay on a fine show.
Mead a-plenty we did swig,
fumbling her curves in some juggled jig;
as we laughed, sang and made merry the meeting.

Hey-ho, Honey, hey, over the hills we will play,
hey-ho, sings the honey bee, come fair maiden
and dance with me.

I fell to the grass, forgettin' mi sorrow,
a long-lasting smile, nay I'd forget, nor tomorrow.
With me at least her task was done
but she will not stop till the setting of the sun.

Hey-ho, Honey, hey, over the hills she will play,
hey-ho, sings the honey bee,
thank ye fair maiden for dancing with me."

Eventually Gam purposefully strode - because he was that sort of a person - into the outskirts of Frostcross and headed down a stone-flagged track between ramshackle buildings. He cast his eye over the outskirts and decided that *dregs* were a better description of the fringes of the settlement. Then he saw the sign naming the lane Rotten Row, and agreed that was far better - it was total, abject, wrist-slitting dereliction.

A wagon clattered over rough cobbles, its contents of salted meat and eggs on its way to the pass through the Montasp mountains - known as the Shepherd's Pass - which eventually led to the nearest city of Cheth Chandor. As far as he knew it was the only way through the mountains and quite a journey at that, one that Gam detested with about the same conviction as he now shared with his Brothers at the Abbey whom had described Frostcross as a seaside retreat!

He had particularly disliked the dangerous Devils Elbow, thusly named after the fearsome drop off the corner of the winding track. The only thing it did in the regions favour was that it kept this peninsula of Barrowdale quite a secluded and remote location.

Barrowdale was littered with ancient barrows, tombs and stone cairns - especially a region north-west of Frostcross that Gam had skirted on the way to the Chapel. A prominent standing stone was known locally as the Oakstone and it was awash with myths about its origin. Gam had remembered when researching Barrowdale in the Tinhallow Library that long-forgotten tales told of an ancient secret lost under its foundation stone - an ancient relic from a fallen empire. The Oakstone was aligned at the highest point of a hill, where the east sun rose and on a direct line to an opposite hill where a largely intact chambered cairn known as Scarpel Rock sat.

Nodding how-do-you-do's to a few friendly farmers and meeting hard stares of lesser savoury folk, the portly Friar at last arrived at what he thought was his destination and what he believed to be the local Ale-house. The sound of drinking, laughing and horsing around - as only bullish and hard-working farmer types could - came to his ears.

The Fool's Nook Inn he had been told, now exactly remembering the persuasive words of a fellow Brother back at the Abbey; 'the upstanding centre of the community, a warm place to wait out any bad weather and enjoy companionship, cheer, song and most of all, good ale.' Staring as he did now at the bleak, weather-worn walls, missing sign and debris littered pathway, Gam guffawed at his kin's remarks and the wind took away the curses falling from his lips so fast that the gods themselves couldn't hear. It was becoming obvious that his fellow Brothers had been taking the piss! And he heaved a sigh accordingly.

He wasn't the most eloquent and well-mannered of clergy but that was his commonly raised background shining through like some rough diamond. It was that tough childhood that gave him his battle-hardened attitude and abrupt mannerisms that perhaps his fellow, more affluent, monks despised and thusly sought to trick him where possible. When it came down to it he considered himself quite a cheerful sort and it really did take an awful lot to put him in a stormy mood.

Gam pushed open the heavy wooden door and the first thing that met him was the smell; stale sweat. He wrinkled his nose and pressed on in and then, to his relief, the scent of ale took over and he paced towards the bar area where he caught the occasional waft of vomit.

The place seemed quite lively for the time of day and though naturally a dark inn with only small, high-set windows, there were plenty of oil lamps fixed to wooden beams.

In the space of heartbeat he was presented with three breasts - a pair from a neighborly whore offering a quick fumble and tumble upstairs, and the other one, inadvertently, from a lass little past her teens and little passed her alcohol limit too.

Gam managed to smile and move the fun-loving prostitute onto another patron and then cover the young girl's privacy as she fell unconscious on the padded bench at the booth. Having got that out of the way he awkwardly hobbled onto a rickety bar stool, sighed with the relief the seat gave and re-adjusted a large ornate hammer hanging across his back, nestled next to a leather pack, bedroll and more importantly, his mead-filled wine skin and empty ale keg. If friends could be inanimate objects then these last five items were best buddies and they accompanied him everywhere.

At present nobody was tending bar but with what he had witnessed so far, it didn't surprise him in the least.

A form of cheesy string was offered with the ale, not for tying naked friends to table legs. However, judging by the amount strewn around the place, the latter was obviously more popular. Gam busied himself with reading a hastily scrawled lunch menu propped up on the sticky counter of the bar, whilst all those around him got merrily sloshed.

Brimy Kitty - a Frostcross special! We coat thick slices of sea cat with a peppery batter and fry until golden brown. Enjoy the steaks dipped in prawn gravy, with a side of a dried seaweed and variety cabbage salad. We recommend either the spicy mead to compliment your meal or the Frosty Shadowaxe Ale and that's *real* ale, no wet wringings of a soggy cloak here!

Wyvern Loaf - No, its not real dragon meat! We mold spiced ground beef into a Wyvern-shaped baking mold and bake in the oven until sizzling throughout. Then we unmold your creature onto a bed of lightly buttered corn bread 'coins'. It's as big as a paladin's ego!

The Meddle's Delight - Jade fungus from Barrowdale's very own marsh is mixed and sautéed in lime butter until tender and served on our mixed-leaf salad drizzled with pear vinegar and sprinkled with sea salt and cracked black pepper. Toasted wholemeal bread, dipped in honey is served on the side. It's tastier than trail rations! Wash it all down with a flute of the pricey but invigorating chilled water, fresh from the Pixie Pools.

In the city most of the weedy fops who frequented the eating houses were satisfied with an olive each, a small slice of some rare fowl and a thumbful of cold sherry. But Gam was not so easily sated and he was pleased to see that the portions looked to be brimming.

"I'll bring you a glass of iced mead while you make your decision," said an unexpected voice and Gam lowered the menu to gaze into the red and sweaty features of what he presumed was the Innkeeper appearing in the doorway.

"Bardon's the name friend," he began, wiping podgy fingers on his apron. "Any of those gastronomic delights take yer fancy?"

"To be honest Bardon, think I'll just have a tankard of your best ale if it's all the same to ye." replied Gam, flashing a warming smile as his great sausage fingers tried to be dainty about picking up delicate fungi bar snacks.

"Whatever you want stranger, best Barrowdale brew," Bardon stopped. "I thought it was a sin for you lot to drink?"

"Not me, like to drink till I can't think."

"Fair enough," said Bardon, smirking, as he began to fill a pitch-lined leather tankard. "What brings ye to our little community of Frostcross? And what moniker do ye go by?" he asked, indicating to the few patrons seated around the taproom. Gam could make out farmers, fishermen, maybe the odd explorer or adventurer.

"Name's Gam and I hail from Tinhallow. I plan to re-open the chapel on yonder hill," he exclaimed looking pleased with himself. He quickly cast his eyes over the room at his announcement, it had been loud enough for most to hear but no one looked up or seemed interested. The only person who was vaguely looking his way was a surly looking dwarf in the corner smoking a long pipe. Gam turned back to Bardon, not allowing himself to be deflated.

"Ah," replied Bardon, handing over a frothy-headed tankard which Gam accepted gratefully and took a long sip from. "That be interestin' to 'ere, we've been without a Minister for nay on several seasons now - glad to be makin' your acquaintance."

Gam lowered the tankard and burped a big, wheaty burp, "likewise. Though it may be a time before I can get the chapel settled and ready. The bad weather's n'alf taken it's toll! The roof's in bad need of repair and within, well, from what I can make out, needs a good clear out, as does the adjoining cottage."

"The weather sure do get mighty rough round these parts. It's not uncommon to experience a whole season's worth of weather in one single day!" replied Bardon, wiping down the bar.

Gam nodded and continued, "there are all manner of chains and locks to get by too, it's trussed up like a pheasant-on-the-fire. Say, you have rooms here don't ye? Think I best take one till I have the place in order."

Bardon suddenly looked very pleased. "Aye and you're more than welcome, of course. Just six silver crowns a night, includin' morning-feast to stay in this humble den of debauchery!" chuckled Bardon, raising his arms to proudly indicate his surroundings.

"Hmm," sighed Gam. "Perhaps a man of the cloth shouldn't stay in such a setting..." Gam looked to Bardon, eyes wide, eyebrows furrowed in mock innocence. "O look, I'm a Friar, one doesn't have many crowns. How about we barter? Or I could say a prayer for ye – that's got to be worth a bit?"

"Make it five then," came a resigning tone.

"Done," came the swift reply.

Bardon smirked, "Tis a hard bargain but it would be a shame to set off on the wrong foot. I can see I'll have to watch out for ye Brother Gam."

"Tell me," began Gam, yarfing down the tankard's contents all at once - it was sure better than that Rotgut they brewed at the Abbey. He handed the empty receptacle back over to the Innkeeper for a re-fill. Bardon eagerly took it, certain he could make up the discount on the room in ale-coin alone. "A general question I know, but as it's my first time in Barrowdale – just what is it like 'round here?"

Bardon handed over the brimming tankard and let out a long breath, "well, it's pretty much a crofters land now. Folk work the land, either crops or livestock and then take their produce to the city Cheth Chandor every few lunar cycles. A Daleman's life is a hard and lonely affair."

"Be there any Frostcross militia? Or men-at-arms to defend the harbor?" asked Gam, a little concerned. He had heard of too many pillaged and burned-out chapels by pirates in his time.

"Nah. Though the farmers be all pretty handy. Those that hunt are good with bow, woodsmen with the axe, and so forth. They're a hardy bunch, but we don't have any professional soldiers if that's what yer mean - though I think Thesden over there used to serve. But it's pretty darn quiet round these parts now. Pirate activity has been down – they know there's nothing of value here! And there's not much in the way of predatory animals or Orc raids anymore, they all stopped in mi Granpappy's time. The Montasp mountain range does a good job of keeping the wild things out!"

"I did see some old earthworks and a ruined fortification on the way here, near Scarpel Rock," offered Gam.

"O aye, left over from some long-lost civilization, the same that probably left the Dale covered in the Barra's that yer see.

Dalesmen in mi great Grandpappy's time rebuilt them but again they fell into disrepair."

Bardon suddenly looked to his right, aware that a nearby hook-nosed patron had finished his drink. The Innkeeper lifted a large clay jug.

"Folk keep to themselves and 'ave settled 'ere to get away from the hectic life of the city," Bardon lowered his voice, "like Thesden over there who I mentioned. Originally a farmer who had been recruited into the Chandorian Militia after he was observed in a bar brawl and pressed into signing up," he chuckled, "apparently, the officer had been so impressed with his talent he had *recruited* him there and then, eventually, bored with that, he became a treasure seeker ."

Gam glanced nonchalantly over to the man and observed a glaive pole-arm propped up against the bar. He could imagine the man as a charming rogue with his blond hair and dark-blue piercing eyes. He would bet that he had conned many a deep-pocketed, desperate manor-wife out of a small fortune.

Bardon must have been thinking the same thing as he then added, in even quieter tones, "I understand it were 'ow he bought his farmstead up yonder at Lon-Ban quite recently."

Bardon now turned to Thesden at the other end of the bar, "not been 'ear that long have ye Thesden?"

The Rogue turned to face Bardon - taking a glance at Gam - and agreed, "Not that long Inn keep."

"This is Gam, Thesden, 'e's gonna open the Cra-" Bardon suddenly faltered and stopped himself from referring to the building as he usually labeled it, "...chapel!" He winked at Gam realising he had made a naff job of covering his gaffe.

"Good to hear," said Thesden in a smooth voice, glossing over Bardon's blunder, "and its good to make your acquaintance Minister Gam."

"I say, are ye related to the Mortlakes of Cheth Chandor - ye have the same nose and look mighty similar!" Asked Gam initially taken back.

Thesden smirked, "that's not the first time I've heard that. But alas, no. Well, unless I'm the offspring of some noble's dalliances with common totty!"

Gam tittered. That wasn't as far fetched as the Rogue may have thought. Words of the Mortlake's impish practices had even penetrated the thick, sanctified walls of Tinhallow.

"Would ye like that mead now?" asked Bardon, noting Gam's empty tankard again and tempting Gam with a drink worth just a little more coin.

"Ah, a spot of pretty tipple that. Mead, mead, from the honey bee, how I long to drink thee-"

"I'll take that as a yes!" Bardon interrupted before Gam got into full choral swing.

The elegant mead flute disappeared into giant hands evolved for grasping weighty war hammers and wringing the necks of buzzards and scoundrels alike, its contents drained in a single slug. Gam indicated a large horn beaker to be filled with the sweet liquid instead. Bardon did so, topped up Thesden's and then began to wander towards a nearby patron dressed in black robes but continued to murmur to Gam, "this is Gutiso Wimplemunch, he runs the local provision store and stables in Frostcross." Without asking, the Innkeeper re-filled a small receptacle in front of Gutiso with the nectar liquor.

Gutiso grimaced, screwing up his gaunt features in disgust, which, added with his hook nose, long black hair - complete with vaguely pointed ears that protruded from his straight hair - made him look quite the ugly fellow. Gutiso was tall and looked uncomfortable at the table with his knees about his ears. His table jumped and bounced like a Ouija board as he desperately folded his long limbs into a more comfortable position.

Thesden bent his head toward Gam and explained quietly that though Gutiso Wimplemunch ran the only store, it was as an alchemist where his love really lay. He then proceeded to tell Gam that the upkeep of the store suffered because of it. Apparently he lived with his sister, Lynessa, who had recently gained employment as a Nanny to three children from the city. In Bardon's absence Thesden went on to point out another local.

"That's Grim," said the Rogue, nodding toward the dwarf in the corner. "Local miner, stern sort a fella, never says much."

Gam peeked at the dwarf he had noticed before - he really did look quite aloof. He also looked very old for a dwarf, maybe four hundred winters, not that Gam had any experience with dwarven lifespan. Heck he had never even met a dwarf before and realised he was staring several moments longer than was polite. But the dwarf just seemed to stare back when his gaze wasn't lost by the thick pipe-weed smoke lazily seeking the ceiling. His beard was long, partly plaited and reached down to somewhere below the table he was seated behind, his hair was similar and shone the rich colour of beaten bronze.

"O Thesy, I'm having such a dull time of it, fancy brightening up mi day?" Suddenly came a voice and Gam realised it was the lady who he had met earlier flashing her assets. She draped herself over Thesden's shoulder. He looked to Gam, "Well, never one to disappoint. Lead the way Tith. Excuse me Brother Gam; do say a prayer for me."

"O, I don't think ye'll need that kind o' support," Gam retorted, eyeing the buxom lass's heaving breast. "The wolf and the Lamb. I see it all the time, the wolf and the lamb," Gam chuckled in a low voice, glancing after the wolf as she lead her new playmate up the staircase, "be gentle on him lass!"

Bardon headed back for the bar area after replenishing Gutiso's drink, snickering to himself. Gam noticed he carefully skirted the dour dwarf, avoiding his table completely.

***

The fingers holding the slim balcony rail were long and delicate. Tith stared over the rugged landscape and rust-coloured heath lands from the attic bedroom on the top level of the Fool's Nook Inn which had now become her own room. She had dressed the room to look quite glam, in a blowsy, common sort of way. She ran her fingers across the top of the rusting rail and back to a thick veil that hung across the doorway, adjusting it behind her as she glided back into the room to stand in front of Thesden who reclined on an old but still plush couch.

She stood in front of him, the fire at her back, her figure outlined provocatively through her thin muslin under-dress. Her dress was already hanging discarded over the changing screen. She knew how much Thesden appreciated her lovely body. The figure on the couch stirred and a smile formed on his handsome, observing face.

"You do like to tease," he said stretching from his relaxed position facing the fire.

Tith laughed, how she treasured this man and how she loved to tease him. Over the cold winters they had found friendship, trust and warmth in each others arms. The relationship worked well, he was not bothered by her questionable vocation and she greatly respected his skills.

She was beginning to care for him dearly and she had already offered to give up her work and had asked him to move in with her under the safety of the Inn's roof. Not that he needed it; he was quite adept at looking after himself. In fact he would often disappear for several ten days at a time, either trips to sell wares in Cheth Chandor or exploration by land or sea.

"Tith. Is everything alright?" he asked quietly, slowly leaning forward from his stretching position.

"Yes, fine, I was just thinking." She faltered slightly and paced back out to the balcony. Thesden in pursuit, "Aye and I know what you're thinking."

Tith turned, betraying surprise, her chestnut eyes wetter than normal. She bit her lip innocently, realising Thesden had come to know her better than that.

"You guessed?" she asked, accepting his strong arms around her, sheltering from the chill sea wind.

"Of course, I know you better than that Tithy but I'll be just fine in Lon- Ban," he smiled warmly and hugged her fiercely. She couldn't help but smile and feeling safe in his arms, glanced down to a simple, ivy reclaiming courtyard and barn below the balcony. Her mind, however, was not on flora, fauna or architecture; it was on the tall, striking man behind her. She reached out, idly following the handsome metal ivory relief that wound the balcony's rail, remembering all those sleepless nights when Thesden had been away and she could not tear him out of her mind, when her body felt empty and overheated and cried out for his.

She felt the warmth from his muscular arms, embracing her from behind, and she knew what was going to happen between them as surely as she knew she loved him. Under the slate grey sky their eyes met, the balcony veil drifted up in the wind to caress their wrapped bodies.

Shattering tenderness swept through her and she closed her eyes, leaning back against him. Thesden bent his head and turning her in his arms, brushed his lips against hers, until finally, kissed her. Tith felt no shame when her thin gown slid down around her hips and Thesden scooped her up into his arms. Still kissing he carried her away from the balcony and over to the double cot. Tumbling her to the cool sheets he passionately kissed her, dropped between her naked legs and grasped her warm thighs.

Over the sound of her gasping moans they did not hear the exclamation of 'Murder!' and the heavy breathing of the vocalist running toward the inn.

***

Bardon topped up Gam's drink without prompting and the Friar muttered something about 'riding the mead hog to the abyss and back again,' as the heavy front door banged open and most of the patrons paused in their conversations to regard a new interloper.

"Murder! Murder!" cried a man that Gam took to be a Fisherman judging by the smell that arrived in his wake. He breathlessly padded up and propped himself against the bar as the patrons gathered around.

"Murder! What ye talking about Ervan?" said Bardon, holding up the jug of mead to the Fisherman. He waved a definite no whilst catching his breath.

"I found old Jonah on the field track near the Shoremeet and he was d..dead, he's been murdered!"

The throng fell into loud exclamations and gossiping and so Gam naturally stepped up to take order. He noted Ervan's breath was like a fox after a night on the bins.

"Firstly, are ye sure he was dead?"

"Well, he wasn't breathing and 'e 'ad two holes in his back," announced Ervan to the Inn.

"Sounds kinda dead," retorted a fellow fisherman in monotone.

"Why is everyone so sarcastic round here?" said Gam under his breath and stepping out of the Fisherman's gasping cone of contagion, "who would ye normally contact in such a situation?" he enquired to the Frostcross crowd.

"Why, Ardd." replied Bardon, rubbing his double chin in thought.

Gam sighed, "the old deceased cleric?"

"Aye, the same!" replied Bardon, "It has always been the priest that investigated such like. I told yer, not much crime."

Every single one of the patrons turned to regard Gam and it went very, very quiet. Someone had to state the obvious and it was Bardon, "quite fortuitous you arrived t'day."

Gam gazed into the expectant faces of the mass assembled around him, "Well, it looks as though my predecessor has volunteered me from beyond the grave!" He finally voiced. He had always fancied himself as a bit of a sleuth, "I suppose I could do that."

Ervan and his cohorts visibly relaxed - the problem had been passed on. He went onto account how he had found Jonah, sprawled in the mud of the track with the two wounds in his back. When Gam had asked after the victim, Bardon filled him in on the old sea dog known as Jonah the Lidless.

"Who do you think could have done this?" Ervan went onto exclaim, "we all know each other pretty well and there have been no strangers 'bout."

"How well do we *really* know each other?" piped in Gutiso at this point, looking suspiciously at everyone assembled.

"I don't think we need to go there," said Gam draining his mead, "I need to take a look at the body, where be this Shoremeet?"

"Your suddenly very quiet Bardon, everythin' alright?" enquired Ervan looking to the Fool's Nook Innkeeper. Bardon looked quit pale, like he had spotted a Sea Spectre.

"Those green, piercing eyes," he whispered.

"What was that?" prompted Gam.

"There was a stranger, first thing this very morn, 'e caught me unawares outside, asking after Jonah – he had his walking-stick!" exclaimed Bardon, obviously still a little shaken and rubbed the seaman's tattoo upon his lower arm. He turned and spoke directly to Gam, "Jonah was 'ere yester-eve too but took off in a 'urry. I thought it funny as he didn't wait for the rain t' stop."

"Hmm. How did this stranger look?" asked Gam.

"'e was wearin' traveling leathers and a brown tricorn – I just remember those green eyes..." he trailed off. Gam nodded.

The only individual that he had witnessed being less than cordial was this Grim the dwarf. As he considered this character he casually glanced towards the corner of the tap room but the dwarf was no longer there. Gam made a mental note to enquire what took the dwarf away from the inn in such haste after the arrival of such appalling news. He re-shouldered his hammer and went to make for the door.

"If ye see this green-eyed fellow again, let me know in all due haste, likewise, if Grim, or whatever his name, appears. O, and another thing Bardon, an Acolyte from Tinhallow should arrive t'morrow-morn with the rest of mi belongings and will require a room also."

The Innkeeper nodded frivolously.

"If ye catch the killer, I have a big pit!" Bardon piped up, speaking his mind.

"Um, ok, thanks, I'll remember that." came the reply.

Bardon looked happy.

"Strange sort of chap wouldn't you say?" intoned Bardon to Ervan, watching the portly Friar leave.

"I dare say he thinks the same of us."

CHAPTER TWO

27th Noon, Lunar Cycle of the Cursed Constellation, 978 Winters.

Gam stooped down to examine the footprints and depressions in the muddy soil. They were of a smallish boot and uneven in depth, signifying either a child or small man with a probable limp. It certainly suggested these were Jonah's footprints. He glanced down the track to a stile and followed the footprints that led up to it. He noticed an area where the mud was badly disturbed and the prints were formed in a chaotic pattern and he spied several hand prints. He guessed this was where the old man had either fallen, was pushed or - as Gam then noticed a spot of blood - received his first wound. Gam climbed the stile gingerly and noted more blood wiped on the wooden post. He reached down the other side but lost track of the prints. He widened his search but first rested his pack and supplies on a small rock and rubbed his shoulder soothingly.

He searched the whole blasted surrounding area of the stile but couldn't find any footprints on its southern side. Scratching his head Gam re-climbed the stile and carefully re-examined the footprints. It just didn't make sense, if Jonah was killed at this point - and the lack of further foot prints certainly indicated that - then where was the body? Ervan had revealed that Jonah was lying next to a stile but Gam had assumed it was another one further up the pathway when the body clearly wasn't in sight here.

In a renewed and careful examination of the footsteps he saw that there were a few light depressions in the soil leading to an old weather-beaten tree, maybe ten paces away. Either Jonah had tried to cover the fact that he had gone to the tree, or he had approached and withdrew carefully and light of foot. But why?

Gam drew near to the tree gazing over the area. Now accustomed to the tell-tale marks, he could see that the prints simply went up to the tree and back. The tree was very gnarled and probably dead, there was no foliage on its rough branches. He did notice an area of shadow at the crook of two boughs and though he couldn't quite see, straining on sandaled tip-toes, he managed to thrust his hand into the space, using the weight of his hammer upon his back to balance him as he strained. Grasping around in leaves and bits of bark he realised there was nothing there. Funny he thought, why else would Jonah have approached the tree at this point? As he settled his balance from the stretch he glanced down so as not to trip on one of the knobbly roots coming out of the ground and noticed a piece of parchment nestled between two of the thick roots. Frowning, he bent over to pick it up when he suddenly heard a noise akin to a rustling bush. He would have naturally thought it as the wind, except that the sound came as the wind died. The rustle had made him jump and he was certain he felt eyes upon him - the hairs on the back of his neck standing to attention. Instinctively, he dislodged the hammer on his back and it fell to the side and his waiting grip, he had it up and ready to swing in an accomplished heart beat.

"Who's there?" The rustling had ceased and Gam waited patiently for several breaths before repeating his hail. Still nothing.

Merry Badger Brock, a playing in the meadow,
running through the foxgloves, spies a portly fellow,
flushed are his features, all busy and a bustling,
brown robe sweeping, sending leaves a rustling.
Picking through the gorse, looking and a fiddling,
being o so thorough, like washing after widdling.

Gam began working his way around the twisted tree and approach the low-lying scrub and gorse bushes beyond, staying as quiet as possible and not taking his eyes off the bushes. That was probably an error as his foot caught a knobbly root and he tripped. For the size of his portly frame he did an outstanding job off steadying himself and avoided crashing haphazardly. He staggered, as in a bizarre dance, and avoided one of the bushes, momentum carrying him over it instead. He struggled to make the best out of the situation and turned the fall into a launch, hammer extended out in front. He landed hard and succeeded in scaring the wits out of a small badger which yelped and disappeared off across the meadow. He breathed a sigh of relief and stood, picking bits of gorse out of his robes.

"Big wild monster," he grumbled to himself, not referring to the lack of one in the badger's place but himself. He returned to the knotted tree and picked up the parchment, unfolding it carefully as it was still quite damp.

Drawn hastily in ink, which in places had run, was what appeared to be a crude map. It revealed many small circles, a few dotted circles, a black oblong - which was inked in - and one large circle. A medium circle - again different in size - had a small *X* marked inside. It didn't mean anything to Gam and he turned over the browned-paper to see if there was anything on the reverse, but alas, there was not. He turned it back over and studied it again.

"Nope, haven't got a clue." He exclaimed, somewhat despondent. He nearly discarded it but realised it must be of some significance. Presumably, Jonah had attempted to hide it within the tree. But why? To keep it from his pursuer? Was it in fact why he was killed?

Too many questions bounced about his addled brain. He would need to sit, contemplate and indulge in a dram or two. Where was the body? It hadn't been that long since Ervan had discovered it. Had the killer returned? Gam's mind insisted on returning to the dwarf, Grim, who had disappeared sometime around the moment that Ervan had arrived at the inn with the news of Jonah's murder - a very suspicious occurrence in light of this latest development. And what of the green-eyed stranger that was so interested in finding the old sailor? Things just didn't tally up and he wondered who he could confide in and trust.

As he reclaimed his pack he decided he daren't tell anyone at present. He tucked the map into a deep pocket within his robe, if only he knew what the drawing meant? It was undoubtedly the only damned clue he had and, therefore, understanding it was his first task.

Not wishing to journey back to the Inn just yet, Gam decided to take a stroll and mull over the recent tumultuous events. He walked a gentle track that wound up to a cliff overlooking the fearsomely rough spray of the Sea of Gold Lightning as it crashed into the cliffs below. The pebbly path then meandered for a short distance adjacent to a thick set of brambles exploding with large red and black berries. Gam stopped on the high crest and turned inland surveying the area. He could just make out the chapel perched on the hill overlooking Frostcross now lost and nestled within the valley and then to beyond where the eerie but peaceful barrows were most prevalent. The tall, single mount of Iron Peak was just visible further inland and the hoary-russet Montasp Mountain Range afar and ominous on the horizon.

Barrowdale was ruggedly beautiful, an ancient land lost in time. The clean air was positively bracing and a far cry from the narrow city streets of Cheth Chandor where he had grown-up. Gam remembered those times well, as a near starving child on the streets of the slums and poor district, fighting for survival. The stink of the gulleys, always flowing with effluent, the rats, mobs and worse.

The day he was plucked from the streets by an old monk from Tinhallow was a god's send and he always took it as such. Especially when news filtered through to him, when in his secluded tutorage, of the premature demise of a former young chum.

The wind picked up a little and distracted him from his thoughts, the sound of the waves prevailing once again. He continued inland along the pathway where eventually it began to be less apparent and the stones scattered into a grassy track meandering around a small wood - their tangled depth redolent of nettles and fungus. To the other side of the disappearing track was a copse of silver birch trees and as Gam drew close, a gust of wind lifted a handful of small pages and dispersed them across the grass. Fortunately, Gam was close now and he instinctively plunged his foot on top of them before they could scatter. Nearby, amongst the trees, a flattened area of longish grass signalled to Gam - as a former adventurer - that this had been a camp spot. Inspecting the handwritten pages he began to read.

Greetings to you, whomever you may be. A friend to have been perhaps, if we should ever have met under better circumstances.

My name is Bethe Arryn and this is the account of my life as it has been for near on two lunar-cycles now, a life that one would never have imagined. I scrawl it here, as clear as I can remember, the adventures of the Tralleign family, that is my sister Yssara Wellisa, my brother Cordale Kethren and myself.

We live at the southern tip of Barrowdale, and thus so, our adventure begins…

25th Morn, Lunar Cycle of the Cursed Constellation,
1189 Winters.

Our respectable father is currently serving the lords of Cheth Chandor, far from our shores. He is a bodyguard to Lord Degarle, ever since saving his life. Before then he was a Master at sea, serving on the Chandorian Militia-ships, an equivalent to Captain, or so Cordale explains, and since has been commissioned by the Lord to act as an explorer. For the honour of saving our esteemed Lord Degarle father was granted land - a lovely old cottage and a small farmstead here in Barrowdale. We are a simple honest family and have never owned anything to the likes of this. Father was initially embarrassed to live in this finery and it is now only a few ten days that we have resided here.

We moved into this cottage expecting to be able to spend some time together as a family. Father said that since mother died he has been away from home far too often and he desired to put that right. However, a message arrived on the first night summoning father to Cheth Chandor - the Lords had need of him. I did not want father to go, I miss him terribly. But he is a loyal and honourable man and does what he must.

Father left Lynessa, our new nanny in charge. She lives in Frostcross and is also attending to a recently stricken Aunt. I do not believe she has been here as much as she should since father left.

Father told us to stay away from the dangerous settlement and to stay clear of the Barrows at Scarpel Rock. Many a superstitious folk live round here, those that believe in the *Earth* magic and the like. Father calls them witches and worse. Good religious folk like ourselves are to stay away from folk such as them. The Tinhallow Witch-finders will catch up with them sooner or later he says. That does not stop us from exploring our new surroundings though, and Cordale often leads us out into the grounds. Just yester eve we followed a terrible clamour to a group of beech trees where many large nests rested in their bows. Ysara said it was a heronry when she finally observed the large birds; my sister is very clever when it comes to all things of nature. We then spied with fearful astonishment that under the trees lay great eels, which had fallen from their nests. It was a scary sight and Ysara and I ran back to the house, not stopping once. Cordale, reacting like some great warrior lashed out at the vile, slippery creatures with a big stick.

Most of the time, with Lynessa absent, it is just Ysara, Cordale and I. Well, and Balthy too. Balthy is a small, affectionate little animal with golden fur. Father gave him to us to look after as our very own pet. He brought him back from his last trip to realms afar. With his golden coat he is worth his weight in gold to us. I had never seen a little animal like him before and Ysara was extremely taken with his curious behaviour, Cordale calls him an overgrown vole, but then, he's just a bullyboy.

The event with the eels had excited us into exploring more and this morning after a lovely breakfast of freshly baked bread and jam, Lynessa revealed that she would not be able to be with us today, so with that, we decided to venture out and carefully explore the old farm grounds, hoping to view a pony, small bear or wild boar.

I am very keen on exploring the old stable building and I know Ysara is keen to visit the small paddock, with it's little duck pond and rickety old fence. Cordale, however, is keen to explore the dark, dense wood at the end of the paddock. Ysara and I are not so keen to look there after father's words, but I expect he will lead us there nonetheless. I'll stop writing for the moment as Ysara has arrived to say Lynessa has left and Cordale awaits us in the herb garden, I am sure it is to be a most exciting day…

25th Eve, Lunar Cycle of the Cursed Constellation,
1189 Winters.

We are now together and spending the night in the small bedroom chatting excitedly of our days exploring. Lynessa has not come back as yet, though she normally always returns before nightfall. I am not sure I mind though. We have had a glorious day exploring the old farm together and I think we are ready to spend a night alone.

When we explored the old stable building we came across a stray dog that has set his home up in the bales of hay at it's rear. I am not sure what breed of dog he is. Ysara thinks he might be a mongrel, but either way he has a beautiful coat of black, velvety fur, large dark wistful eyes and is strong and true in stature. I think we made him jump when we first saw him; no one has been out to the stable since we moved in and goodness knows how long the cottage was unoccupied before us. Ysara ran back to the house and brought a clay bowl of water and the left over scraps from the pheasant the night before and set them down in the middle of the stable. We stepped back so as not to appear threatening and the dog emerged from his hiding place to feed. After, he visibly relaxed and let us touch and stroke him. When father returns we will ask if we can take the dog in and look after him, but for now we will feed and water him everyday. We have named him Moonfar, as he is so black even the moon does not seem to illuminate him.

Moonfar accompanied us while we played in the paddock; he enjoys leaping over the old fence for sticks Cordale throws for him.

For dinner we greedily ate the last of the farmhouse cake and muffins that Lynessa had baked, perhaps she knew she would not be back and that is why she had made so many.

It is very humid this eve and the sea is very still, we opened all the windows upstairs before climbing into bed. Cordale dragged in a cot from our bedroom so we could all be together; he says he wants to tell us a story before bed. Ysara and I jumped into bed and pulled the covers up and listened to him intently.

'At my Schooling House, just outside Cheth', began Cordale. 'Remember we received the local old priest from Tinhallow? Do you know why that was?'

Ysara and I shook our heads.

'It all happened on the night of Raelans Constellation when our Master Savant, Ritic Vilan, was instructing late with an apprentice, when tragedy ensued and evil descended upon the school like a heavy, suffocating blanket.

The next day - Raelans Wake, that is - we were all sent to the main hall where the local cleric was waiting for us, he had us sit and wait until all the pupils were joined. Our curious whispers were silenced more than once whilst we waited. It was unusual to have the local priest visit us, all assemblies were normally taken by Master Ritic, striding the stage clenching his precious manual. It then struck us that the winding staircase up to the viewing tower had been locked and sealed that morn – that door was never, ever closed; indeed one does not even remember it having a door before. I had only noticed the door because I needed to visit the latrine on my way to the hall and taken but a slight detour. Inside I was surprised to find the Master Savant's manual that he carried everywhere with him, it was unmistakable in its roughly bound tan, leather cover. By this time however, I was running late for the hall calling and pocketed it to return to him later. I was still desperate for the latrine.

Anyway, once we were all together and seated, the old cleric began. He took out a large cloth and dabbed his brow, he was nervous and troubled and it only lent more to our curious nature – this must be something serious.

The priest went on to relate the night befores events…''O do come on and tell us,' Ysara teased, as Cordale took delight in pausing.

'I am not sure that I should, replied Cordale in a low murmur, one does not want to be blamed for causing my little sisters a sleepless night', he teased, tickling Ysara. I laughed too and bade him continue.

'All right, my warning is present but not heeded, this is your choice. The events that I am about to relate were never uttered outside the school's enclosure; I doubt if the news even arrived at Mortlake Castle and it certainly did not become general folk knowledge... ever.

The old priest related to us that Jespar, the young apprentice, and Master Savant Ritic had died under tragic circumstances last eve, up in the old viewing tower.

We were all of course terribly shocked and shaken and were sent back to our instruction-rooms with all due haste. However, I was desperate for the latrine and sneaked to the far corridor to visit. Whilst I was inside I heard several Savants conversing about last night's gruesome incident and it was there, sitting on that latrine, that I heard the full grim tale. Apparently, in that old tower, the late Master Savant Ritic took a turn for the worse; they said that demons had selected him in which to cause Cheth Chandor's children great mischief. The Master had turned on poor Jespar, strangling the living breath from him, and... skinning him.'

'S..Skinning him,' muttered Ysara, sinking slightly under the patchwork covers.

'Yes!' Continued Cordale, 'just, like, a, chicken. That was not the worst of it however. When Jespar's kin came to see what was keeping the boy they discovered the Master Savant engaged in some ritual where he danced and skipped around a candle-lit image scribed upon the floor, wearing the young apprentice's skin.

From what I understand, as by this time the Savants were departing the corridor, was that the family flew at Master

Savant Ritic with unmatched anger at seeing the lifeless flesh of their dear son until the Master and poor Jespar's family were all slain. The last thing that I heard before the Savants were entirely out of ear-shot, was that the Chandorian Militia discovered a secret alcove in the old tower, brimming with skulls and bottled internal organs and that his manual, the one he always kept with him, was probably a demonic book of necromantic rituals - an evil handbook if you like. The Savant went on to relate what the Seargeant of the Militia had said and that various writings on the subject revealed that it would have been bound, bound in… human skin.

I of course froze; unable to move for many heartbeats as I remembered, to my utter horror, the very book that they were warning of was in my very pocket, complete with what I previously had assumed was nothing more than a poor leather-bound finish.

I dared not take out and look at the book and confirm the gruesome truth, yet I knew, deep down, it to be true.

The very last comment that the Savant made will stay with me to my dying day, he said, a child of necromancy never, ever, leaves his nefarious tome and will go to any lengths, any lengths, even in the after life to retrieve it…'

I began to shake, I had never heard of such evil. Certainly I had heard folk whisper of sinister goings on, yet to hear this, a first hand account, it scared me more than any of those whispered tales. Ysara was shaking frantically and disappeared under the covers completely.

'T..That was why f..father was called to your school,' she trembled from under the blanket.

Cordale nodded slowly at me. 'And that just leaves me to reveal to you one thing that I have never, ever, dared utter, not even to father.'

I was very curious by this stage, and even Ysara emerged from under the covers.

Cordale took out a small, rectangle shape, wrapped in one of his handkerchiefs and laid it in front of us on the bed. He stared at it for a moment, almost shaking, something that I had never seen my brother do.

'Surely not!' Exclaimed Ysara backing away, 'surely you do not still possess it!' Cordale nodded warily and reached for the book.

'No!' I shouted staying his hand before he could reveal the evil tome, seeing it would only heighten my terror and make the whole tale too fearfully true.

Cordale jumped at my exclamation and fumbled the book, knocking it across the bed toward the window, the kerchief unravelling.

Ysara shouted frantically, dread tinged to her voice, 'what if he comes to reclaim it!'

Cordale dived for the tome, just as the curtains parted and…

'HISSS' came a loud, spine-chilling sound as something began to emerge through the window. The wind had risen in the same instance and a cold chill invaded the room, sending the drapes into a dizzying spin, like dancing robed acolytes.

The palm of my hands went clammy and the hair on the back of my neck stood to attention, a chill gripped at my heart and I fell back onto the bed from the window. Ysara dived under the covers again, whilst Cordale back-peddled away from the flapping curtains, 'It is Master Ritic Vilan!' He cried pointing to the window and falling away, just as a large rat leaped through the opening, hissing evilly.

I had expected to see some chilling apparition enter through the window ready to steal back his necromantic book and however scary this rat was, I found my voice quicker than I would have expected. 'Cordale! Ysara!' I cried, 'it is but a rat!'

Cordale recovered quickly and rose to my side. It was then that realisation hit me and the heavy dread returned to my heart and gripped me in its icy grasp not letting me move. The rat was twice the size to the sewer rats I had seen in Cheth Chandor.

The dark, grey vermin chattered at me with yellow, vicious teeth, its whiskers twitching in anticipation, tail dancing expectantly. It hissed again and locked onto me with almost crimson, ravenous eyes. It tensed, perhaps about to leap at me, but all I could do was stare with morbid fascination at this horrific creature.

Cordale threw out an arm and shoved me into the wall just as the rat leaped. It missed, but I smelt its vile stench as it passed to land on the floor and disappear out onto the landing. I could hear it's deadly, disease-ridden claws scurrying on the wooden floorboards as it descended the staircase.

Cordale grabbed at me and I realised I had my eyes tightly closed and I was breathing heavy and fast.

'Bethe,' he said urgently, 'Bethe, are you all right?'

I opened my eyes and nodded, still a little shocked. 'We must follow it and get it out of the cottage.'

I was still stunned a little by the surprising event, though I nodded in understanding. I looked to Ysara who was emerging from the bed, she had been crying and looked terrified.

'I hope it does not hurt Balthy,' Cordale intoned, reaching for a mop and breaking off the head.

With that comment Ysara steeled her nerves and joined us as we flew out of the room and down the staircase. I am very proud of my sister.

Master Savant Vilan's book laid beneath the window, forgotten in the commotion, yet Cordale's handkerchief had unravelled enough to read its cover; 'Sorceries of the Wraith so shrouded...'

Gam pondered what he had read, strolled over to a smooth rock projecting up amongst the long grass and gently seated himself upon it. "Now let me see, the Wraith huh. That demonology-dabbling pirate-"

Now more comfortable on the sun-warmed rock, he read on.

'...We all hurried down the staircase after the rat, snatching at the post to spin us over the last few steps in all due haste.

'There it is!' cried Ysara who pushed passed myself to reach the ground floor with urgency, she grabbed the stick off Cordale and flew at the rat with rage unbounded. Cordale blurted with surprise at our courageous sister, it was clear that she was trying to scare the rat away down the adjacent corridor – away from where Balthy was.

It worked and we sighed with relief as it disappeared into the Drawing room. Cordale retrieved a broom and large pan from the kitchen and passed the broom to me.

We made our way cautiously down the dark corridor. When we reached the doorway to the Drawing room, all was quiet, too quiet to my mind, something was afoot. Fortunately, the moon was out and shed a pale illumination through the Drawing room windows and Cordale nodded to us both. With cries of surprise and shouts to shock, we leaped into the room. At this point, to our dismay, the moon suddenly went behind a heavy cloud and the room, once again, was in utter darkness.

'Look to the doors!' Cried my sister as she had noticed that which we had not - the large rat had succeeded in prizing open the doors and now to our horror more of its fell kin began to enter. They must have been waiting for the rat to grant them entry all along. This seemed too well organised and intelligent for simple rats I thought, but could not dwell, as the immediate threat was too great - the rats were swarming through.

We backed up to the doorway of the Drawing room, standing three-a-breast, our makeshift weapons clutched tightly in white knuckled fists. The rat-swarm approached us warily like some black, fell blanket, how many their numbers were, I could not tell, they were so closely packed together. Soon we could clearly see their red hungry eyes and their expectant dancing tails. I noticed Cordale look to us with great concern etched into his young face. He took one brave step forward to defend his sisters, but Ysara - who was quite composed - and I, stepped up with him. This was *our* cottage, not the rats!

The lead row of large rats were close, ready to jump. We clutched our weapons and held them aloft, and then suddenly, in those long heartbeats of time, the moon came out again. To our horror it seemed that the rats' heads had an almost man-like quality. At that frightful sight Cordale swung the pan with great vigour and connected with the lead rat knocking it aside. The rats all hissed with what I would describe as rage, they were certain to attack at any moment, when, suddenly a vicious barking noise came from beyond the doors and a jet-black shape launched through the opening to land within the pack of rats, snarling and snapping at the vermin. For a moment we could only discern flashing white teeth, until Ysara cried out, 'Moonfar!'

My sister swung her mop at a rat, knocking it to the side attempting to reach our saviour. Cordale and I shared surprised glances and followed after our sister, swinging broom and pan.

Initially we seemed to be driving the rats away, but, were it me, or were the rats growing in size further? I screamed as now a *huge* rat, had taken a man-like appearance and stood on two legs lifting Cordale up off his feet. My brother was shouting for help and Moonfar responded to my brother's wails spinning and biting into the ratman's thigh. The thing cursed in pain and backhanded the dog away. Moonfar yelped but stood again and backed up to protect Ysara and myself from the twisting and lurching forms of the rats as they all began to turn into... men.

I must admit I screamed with horror, shouting for Cordale as the ratman threw him into the wall, where he lay quite still. Ysara whimpered and subconsciously touched Moonfar at the scruff of his neck. We backed away further into the cold, stone wall, Moonfar snarling viciously at the evil, naked men as they surrounded us - their rat like features still bristling, teeth chittering and piercing red eyes, staring.

'This is it,' breathed Ysara, not wanting to look. I began trembling and dropped to my knees, whimpering for father...'

Gam realised his heart was beating faster and reached for the wineskin and took a swig of mead to calm himself. Drinking back the cool liquid, he replaced the stopper, dabbed his brow with the voluminous sleeve of his robe and turned the page of Bethe's diary.

'...It was then, that what I thought was another ratman stepped through the open doorway to regard its brethren swarming around us. But then the man spoke with a clear strong voice, and I realised with stomach churning relief that this was not another rat man...'

"Thank the gods!" exclaimed Gam and then realised where he was. He glanced around, let himself a slight smile and turned back to the pages.

'...Desist your attack, gutter filth! You will regret the day you rose from the sewers!'

With that the stranger - with lightning quick reflexes - darted forward and ran through one of the ratmen with some kind of long thin blade. The ratman snarled and crumpled into a heap, dead. This drew the other ratmens' immediate attention and they launched themselves at the new stranger. Ceasing this opportune moment Moonfar leaped at the nearest vermin-man and fell on his neck, latching his jaws about it. Ysara grabbed at my arm and forced me up, wiping tears away from her face and pointed to Cordale, still lying unconscious against the far wall and indicated our task.

But then the new stranger, whilst fighting off the ratmen, picked up Cordale and swung him over his shoulder so he could protect the boy, for I noticed several ratmen were sneaking up on my unconscious brother.

Two further ratmen fell to the stranger's blade and Moonfar had tackled another. The vermin creatures began to chitter with either excitement or fright, I could not tell, as more of their number fell.

'Back up the corridor!' The stranger shouted to my sister and I, and we did as he bade, guiding Moonfar with us. At this point I could get a good look at the stranger and studied his tall, handsome features. Longish hair fell haphazardly under a leather tricorn, a black shirt was ripped in many places, as were his breeches and a silver castle icon hung from a thong around his neck. And then I noticed his limp and the blood collecting in a pool where he was fighting the ratmen. He was injured, though I did not remember seeing him get hit by one of the ratmen's clawed hands. This was an older wound that had perhaps re-opened having not enough time to heal properly. The stranger gasped from the pain but did not take his concentration off the task at hand. Another two ratmen fell to his calculating thrusts and as the stranger back-stepped away to join us at the doorway the remaining ratmen gave up, turned tale and fled out into the night.

We all sighed and breathed heavily, the danger had lifted. Yysara beckoned the stranger to lay Cordale from his shoulder. My sister wiped the tears from her eyes and threw down the stick she held so tightly in contempt at the stinking corpses of the rat men.

'Wererats!' spoke the stranger, replying to Ysara's silent request.

'Pardon?' I asked, slowly moving closer to the stranger and half staring at his wound.

'Wererats - lycanthropes, whatever one wants to call them.'

I nodded half heartedly, almost uncaring at what the evil things were.

'What is your name kind sir?' I asked instead. It was the first time the stranger glanced down to me, seeking my eyes. His was of calm intent, just as I remembered our father's after a run-in with a cutpurse in the city. My body froze from his scrutinising gaze, yet I could not tear my eyes from his beautiful green pupils...'

"Green eyes!" Exclaimed Gam, tearing his eyes away from the parchment. His mind immediately snapped back to reality and the investigation at hand and after pausing in thought for a moment, he carried on reading.

'...You are a brave girl,' the stranger spoke, "all of ye." However, he did not steal his gaze from mine. It was then that his expression softened and holding his wounded leg casually, and with little regard from himself, replied to my question.

'Rake is a name that will suffice for me young lady, no other need there be. Trouble may follow ye like a plague if thee knows my given label!'

Before I could protest however, he indicated my comatose brother and told Ysara to help him into the next room where he would soon come and offer aid, but first *Rake* – as he seemed to want to be called, insisted on fixing the doors before he would let me tend to his wounds. As Ysara disappeared down the corridor with Cordale leaning on her, I took in the devastation to our Sitting Room and the shock of the encounter began to sink in and a flurry of frightening emotions swept over me.

'WHY?' I began to sob, why us, what is happening?' I fell to my knees in front of Rake, wiping the tears from my eyes. I felt his hands gently grip my arms and he lifted me to my feet. Looking at his scarred face, he replied in comforting, hushed tones, 'It is not of your making. None of this is a burden to bear. Of morn I will be gone and those creatures after me, I promise it. I am sorry to say my young friend, that it is because of I, ye and yours were set upon. An evil stalks me wherever I roam, and these creatures are its ilk," Rake said, rubbing the cold from my arms in a soothing manner. "I will not let them harm ye again."

I cried but it was with relief this time, not fright. When I looked up next, Rake was leaning heavily against the mantelpiece, he was grimacing and beginning to go very pale. He cast an urgent look to the door and then back to me, clutching his thigh. I recognised then in his eyes, the fear of one who was about to pass out, but at the same time horrified at the prospect when danger still lurked. It was then that Rake collapsed into a heap, his sword stuck - point first - into the wooden floor boards and gently swayed to and fro.

I shuddered and wiped the tears streaming down my face and went to him with urgent haste, it was then that I observed the red eyes glowering at me from the fireplace. I stopped abruptly and backed up as the rat creature emerged from its hiding place and began to stalk towards me. I wanted to stay and help Rake but the feeling rising from the pit of my tummy froze me solid and the overwhelming urge to flee took over. Casting further tears at my predicament, I am ashamed and saddened to say that I fled like a hare down the corridor, leaving Rake alone, helpless, and at the mercy of the dreadful rat.

I am not sure which emotion awakened within me first, fear, anger or relief when I realised that the rat pursued me rather than staying with Rake. I would like to say relief, but here in my diary I can honestly say that I believe it was fear and anger - the thought that I was its target now and not the unconscious Rake.

I emerged from the end of the corridor into a dark lean-to at the rear of the house where Ysara was tending to Cordale on the day bed. My hope was with Moonfar but then, shockingly, I saw what were his little limbs, bloodied and lifeless, sticking out from the doorway.

Ysara had not seen him and she looked to me, at first relieved to see me and then her face dropped to one of dismay when she realised my running was not in relief to be with them but because of the transforming rat that was close on my heels. The ratman hissed with rage and dripped saliva onto the floor boards in anticipation of his catch. In its haste it sent the sideboard and vase crashing to the ground, china and water went everywhere and I screamed, ducking from the flying debris and, inadvertently, avoiding the lunging ratman. It had now completed the transformation to his dirty man-form and landed on all fours to my other side, cutting me off from my sister and brother.

'There isssss no esssscape little one!' it hissed at me and I was taken quite aback as I had never heard any of these vile ratmen speak.

I stepped back until I was pressed up against the wall and I could feel the coldness against my back. The ratman rose up so as to stand on two legs, it stood for a moment gaining its balance and then began to reach out for me and step towards me. I noticed Ysara was frantically looking for some sort of weapon to use against it, but she was running out of time. I could smell its rotten breath as it tentatively stepped towards me.

Just as the thing reached me a curious noise came to my ears, a rolling noise from the floorboards, I glanced up and through my tears could see little Balthy in a glass ball careering toward the ratman at quite a speed. I could not believe my eyes! The little animal was running at full pelt inside and in turn causing the orb to roll extremely fast. I could discern his large and alert dark eyes, bristling whiskers and twitching nose. Surely he was not guiding his ball to strike the ratman on purpose - he was just a small animal? Either way, the ratman saw him coming a moment later than I, and too late at that. Realising the imminent collision I leapt away just as Balthy rammed his glass ball into the ratman - who was already unstable on his two legs - and brought him crashing to the ground in a haphazard heap of flailing arms and legs. I reached down and picked up the glass orb, which luckily had not broken, Balthy was lying upside down inside but he gathered himself up quickly to gaze into my face now that I had lifted him. He gave me such a curious little expression I chuckled out loud, his whiskers twitching in his own amusement.

In the commotion Ysara had found a walking stick and brought it down hard onto the ratman's head and it collapsed back down into an unconscious heap. Without breaking stride she relieved me of Balthy and intoned, 'I told you he was special!'

I nodded enthusiastically after her, still quite bemused by the incident. 'I had put him in the glass orb just after the first rat had attacked in a hope that it would protect him,' said Ysara. It certainly worked and protected us in the process! I replied, hugging my sister.

A weak cough drew our attention to the daybed and Cordale still unconscious upon it.

'What are we to do?' asked Ysara, the fear returning. I was going to answer when Cordale coughed again and then groaned in pain - he was waking.

'Where is Moonfar?' Asked Ysara, still clutching the orb and Balthy who seemed to be observing us with great interest. I revealed the news of Moonfar's passing and she broke down sobbing. Balthy glanced up, large eyes staring after her. At that moment Cordale stirred and fell into a quiet, peaceful sleep.

I then went onto to tell Ysara that which Rake had relayed to me and we then carefully walked the corridor that led us to the Sitting Room, Rake, and - Gods protect us - a ratless room.

26th Morn, Lunar Cycle of the Cursed Constellation, 1189 Winters.

This morn we find ourselves reasonably comfortable in the Sitting room, warming by the fire and with door and windows barred, growing unusually at ease and accustom with the horrific nights events, we looked to Rake to explain this enigma. Cordale joined us at the hearth and together with Ysara - Balthy curled on her lap.

'Why am I here? ye asked me Bethe. I live nearby and I was passing to Frostcross when I heard the commotion. Friends had told me of your father's recall to Cheth Chandor and I knew you were on your own. I am in this gods-forsaken back water because an evil threatens me and has harried me through briar and bog, dogged me through forest, field and fen, chased and tracked me through wood, river and peak, to here. They will not stop until they have laid me and my knowings to rest. Now that ye have lifted your hand against my nemesis, our first task is to get you to safety. A friend of mine will do this.'

'Who is this person?' asked Cordale.

'His name is Dulwin, he is a good friend and comrade tha-'

Gam had reached the end of the text and refolded the torn pages, realising the last date was only yester-morn. He stood and turned in a circle scanning the moorland around him.

"Where are you now young-uns?" he mulled. "I'll say a prayer this eve for your safety in the hands of your new guide, whomever he be." He pocketed the pages with the map, hoping that one day he might just meet this Bethe Tralleign and return them. He decided to head back to the Inn, the hunt for this green-eyed man and the investigation into Jonah's death and subsequent disappearance was unquestionably afoot.

It must have been late afternoon, judging by the failing light as he circled back towards Frostcross, treading the rough, lightly traveled trail that meandered north up the Barrowdale coast. Gam finally arrived back on the cart-track that wound up the picturesque valley adjacent to Frostcross and running parallel to a small river. Soon the track came to a small courtyard of farmhouses on the banks of the river, just beyond them the Friar could make out a little shack and ferry boat, moored ready for use. Tossing the Ferryman a couple of silver crowns he boarded the rickety old craft and waited at its stern whilst the Ferryman signalled to the winch team on the opposite bank to begin hauling it across the river. After a short period of choppy and sick-wracked travel he reached the bank and gladly continued his journey back to Frostcross on foot.

Soon a small wagon pulled by two horses came into view, moving along the stony track. The wagon had seen better days. A lantern mounted on a post to the side of the bench seat swayed as the iron bound wheels crashed over the potholes. Gentle and low tuneful whistling scarcely rose above the clattering horses' hooves. A man, huddled in blankets, stopped his tune when he noticed Gam at the side of the track. At first he stared murderous looks at the Friar and only when Gam waved a cheery hand, did he relax and nod back.

Suddenly, Gam felt a prickling sensation to the back of his neck; something was watching him, something not living. He felt something drawing closer and glanced to either side. Nothing was there.

The wagon had begun to move off and the man continued his tune. Gam controlled his fear and scanned the twilight countryside, it was definitely growing colder and a supernatural eeriness pervaded over the area.

The nearby wagon suddenly surged into motion. Gam watched in disbelief as the horses reared up, terrified, drawing shouts from the occupant. The horses tore through the countryside, leaving the cart-track. One of the horses stepped in a deep hole where the ground had sunk between large tree roots, and went down. Gam heard the snap of breaking bone even over the distance they had gained. The falling horse took down the other animal as well, causing the wagon to slam into both of them and overturn, sending the screaming rider up and under it. When the wagon settled against the ground, neither of the horses moved and the whimpering stopped.

Gam stared after the ruin, shock igniting upon his face at the sudden horrific event. Gam instinctively stepped back and his sandaled foot scuffed loose stone as he kept his eyes firmly fixed ahead - he would not be taken by surprise. He reached for his ornate hammer and after a ten-breath cautiously stepped forward letting his feet search out for a stable footing. At that moment a bitterly cold gust of wind blew into him, tossing the end of his robe like ghosts. Shivering gently, he squinted into the gloom, steadying his nerves. The Friar stared hard; an icy dread seemed to rob him of his free will. There was unquestionably a figure standing in the depths of the darkness of the tree line but it seemed to be lacking its lower body. Gam could clearly see a head, shoulders and arms silhouetted against the bushes, deep red eyes glowing like hot coals that seemed to stare into Gam's very soul. Then the ghostly figure materialised right in front of his eyes.

It was a human girl but one who had been horribly disfigured. Long dark hair clung in matted clumps to a blistered scalp; her once youthful face was horribly disfigured and burnt. Skin had bubbled away in places, including her nose and the rest of her face and neck were blistered badly. The figure continued materialising, that is, down to its waist, and its torso became corporeal, yet Gam suspected that an enchanted weapon would be needed to bring harm to it. He was glad for his hammer and it felt strong and secure in his grasp. However, the ghostly figure made no threatening moves.

"Run from this land..." it rasped in a voice that would have sent an un-experienced Acolyte running for cover.

"Run Brother Gam..." it hissed again. "Only deeeath awaits you here..."

"It knows mi name," exclaimed Gam but under his breath, "that can't be good!"

The figure gave a slow, mournful nod, "run from this land."

"I appreciate your concern but I'm not about to succumb to advice from one who walks beyond death. Why have ye appeared?" Gam asked, studying the spectre.

The spirit waved its blistered hand, attempting to silence Gam's words, it was clearly trying to warn him of something important but it kept looking behind as if hurrying to speak. Gam looked passed the figure to where it was snatching glances but could only see the still trees. "Run from this land." The ghost pleaded.

"Ye must tell me more before ye can expect me to comply. Ye don't want me to stay? To investigate the murder?" Gam asked and then suddenly had a nasty thought, "Are ye Bethe, or Ysara?" He urgently asked, sensing the spectres impending end. But before the spirit could reply, it turned and fled through the trees, crying a deathly wail that covered Gam's skin in ice-cold dread, like that of falling snow on naked skin. He shuddered from the experience deciding that swapping his hammer for his mead was more beneficial. He waited before moving to check the crash site and the unfortunate occupant of the wagon in case the ghost or something worse materialised instead.

Fortunately, nothing did.

***

"So ye have two dead Dalesmen, but only one body - which isn't Jonah's!"

That was the remark that met him at the Fool's Nook when Gam had arrived back at the Inn. It occurred to him that the Inn was aptly named.

After deftly avoiding a detailed account of things with Bardon and a gaggle of flopsies still looking to secure their board for the night with a lonely farmer, he headed up the stairs to his room. He did have time however, to secure a jug of mead as a companion for the night and in doing so had to relay some information. He decided to keep most of the events to himself, including the ghost that had visited him on the cart-track on the outskirts of Frostcross. Revealing *that* somewhat spooky encounter would surely have scared the citizens to the end of their wits – which wouldn't have been that far, or hard, he thought – then chastised himself for being a little unfair. He also had to relay why he had a body with him other than the one he set out for.

The poor farmer who had died so tragically under his wagon was currently locked inside an empty out-building of Gutiso's, from where he could be buried tomorrow.

As he had decided earlier, he kept the map and the diary pages to himself and once he had finished questioning Bardon - who revealed in his absence that neither the dwarf, Grim, or the green-eyed stranger, had returned - he headed upstairs clutching his nightly tipple o so securely.

CHAPTER THREE

28th Morn, Lunar Cycle of the Cursed Constellation,
1189 Winters.

The next morn had arrived quickly enough and Gam had risen with the sun, took prayers and left the Inn early, even if a little bleary eyed and boggy. The morning was dank and grey, but the bitter cold of the previous night had passed in those last cycles of dark before dawn. Heading for the chapel, he was in far better mood for not having to engage in pissy questioning from Bardon.

The raw, blistery wind whistled through the heather and the eerie howl of the ocean reached Gam's ears as he climbed the steep hill to the chapel. He drew his heavy woollen cloak tighter around him, whistling an amorous tune to keep his cockles warm.

Her eyes enflamed and sparkling too,
her cheeks, of all the roses hue.
Lithe and slender a willowy height,
her lips were blooms yet far more bright.
Her breasts two sand dunes or hills of snow,
in which two vivid rubies glow.

Gam glanced to the east where in the distance the grey-brown downs stretched off sloping slowly up to higher wooded slopes, again marching for miles up to the ancient imposing mountains that skirted Barrowdale. The Innkeeper had said as much but the Montasp mountain range separating

Barrowdale from the mainland was an excellent natural wall against marauding Orc bands and brigands - he could see why. Gam stopped to take a breath, surveying the landscape from his vantage point. He hadn't truly appreciated just how many barrows seemed to litter the region. They were everywhere, ancient but still noticeable and perfectly circular.

"Circular?" whispered Gam, he suddenly had an epiphany and quickened his pace for the chapel.

The arched doorway sat at the base of a thick-set oblong tower. Above the entranceway, engraved into the stonework, were the words; 'Hark, all ye. Do you not see how they agree? Then cease, fair folk; why weep ye? See, see, your lord bids you cease, and welcome Love with love's increase.'

After futilely flailing around with the chains on the chapel doors for a good while he at last gained entry, thanks to a strategically placed key above the stone lintel, below the inscription. Again precious time could have been saved if his fellow Brothers had been a little more truthful. However, at least he could now explore his winning idea thanks to the chapel's library.

Furnishings of different periods were crammed into the small aisle-less nave and chancel. It was understated and of a domestic grandeur just like the local noble house of Mortlake who had originally built it before the family had immigrated to the castle adjacent to the mountain city many generations ago.

The walls tilted at odd angles and box pews were jammed into every available space. A small font was tucked down steps under the gallery, surrounded by very old and ornate benches. The gallery itself formed the three sides and set on thick, fluted pillars that were now crusted with cobwebs. The Mortlake pew at the front still had padded, if worn, seats and a threadbare carpet that led up to it. On the wall adjacent to the entrance were what appeared to Gam as striking old memorial plates with beautiful lettering. A few earlier pews crowded the chancel and to the far north, guarded by gates was a small, simple but effective memorial to the Barrowdale fishermen lost in the great storm. Gam padded passed the little colourful memorial feeling humbled at both the loss of life in that storm but also the camaraderie of the Dalesmen that pulled together to fund the memorial, learning this from the plate at its base. It had been sanctioned by the current Lord Mortlake - clearly a family that cared for its less fortunate kinfolk.

Moving passed the last polished pew Gam scuttled down three steps and through an opening that led to a secure door that in turn led to the adjoining minister's cottage and the door to the chapel's library.

***

The stranger cautiously and carefully worked his way around the old stone chapel. He inclined his head to the high-set window, listening out for the return of the fat friar. He craned his neck to the stone window ledge but was unable to glance inside due to the height and the grime on the stained-glass leaded lights. He decided to wait for the Monk to return rather than stalking into an area where he could be trapped, after all he had no idea of the layout of the chapel and he had made it a life rule to never go anywhere that didn't have more than one way out. He had survived thusly, working to such a decree.

He snuck down behind a thick bush, re-adjusting his waxed leather and clasped cloak, fiddling with his tricorn to make sure that he had an unhindered vision of the chapel's only door. With intense green eyes he watched and waited.

His patience was rewarded after he counted two hundred. The thick oak doors abruptly thundered open and the portly fellow half fell through the opening exclaiming. He wrinkled his brow with amusement and almost chuckled with the Friar's buffoonery. He watched and waited for the doors to be re-locked and only then did he make himself known.

Gam turned, a winning smile blossoming from his red features. The chapel had been an absolute mess and exceedingly smaller than he had envisioned but he brushed all that aside, right now he was a happy fellow indeed with his discovery. When suddenly, turning, "why does the devilling-boar-shit-in-the-grass! Where did ye come from and why do ye seek to scare a poor old friar out of his wits!" Gam crudely exclaimed and visibly jumped when a stranger stood from behind the bushes.

The stranger didn't speak for a moment, not that Gam would have seen his lips move from behind the high collared cloak, in fact all that he could see under the tricorn and at this distance was the stranger's piercing eyes. Eyes that were green.

Gam composed himself realising he faced possibly both Jonah's murderer and the Rake character from Bethe Tralleign's diary pages. In the space of a heartbeat he decided to act all the innocent.

"Well good stranger, who are ye and why do ye appear at my door? The chapel is nay open and will not be for sometime I'm 'fraid." Gam used the bluff to weigh up his options, though surely just for being here he must know that Gam was investigating the disappearance of Jonah. Gam thought quickly. He wouldn't have enough time to unlock the doors and re-gain entry into the chapel before the stranger would close on him. No, he would meet this fellow head on if necessary. Few had walked away from his hammer strikes, and those that did, limped. Badly. But somehow this stranger, Rake - as labeled from the child's texts - although trying to give the impression of a menacing individual, wasn't quite pulling it off. "Well, the gull got yer nips?"

The stranger's brow furrowed and judging by his flexing fingers near the hilt of his sword, appeared desperate. A list of questions flooded out in a well-spoken lilt, possible Chandorian in accent.

"Did you find the body? Did you find anything interesting? What have you learnt?" The questions were rapid and urgent. When Gam decided not to answer straight away the stranger prompted him, "Well? What have you learnt? The dead stir Father Gam, this land is no longer safe."

Gam noticed those green eyes and they were pleading. He decided there and then that this was almost certainly the Rake that saved the children and although possibly responsible for Jonah's disappearance, it was not an obvious matter of cruel murder - something about his voice and mannerisms didn't indicate a gruff killer, just a desperate man. Bardon had described a confident individual - what had changed? At first Gam had assumed Rake's questioning was to learn of the evidence that was stacking up against him, but he wasn't so sure now, something else drove his questions. Gam decided to explore a different avenue of inquiry.

"Well, you're as balsy as a buccaneer's stripy breeches, hey? Look, I know ye label is Rake. I know ye helped the Tralleign children against the werecreatures and somehow..."

His words were cut off as suddenly Rake shot an urgent look to his left and made a sprint for the corner of the chapel.

"Hold Rake! I can help but ye must speak with me!" Gam hollered after him as a new voice spoke up.

"Gam! Brother Gam?"

He glanced in the direction of the hail but started to move after Rake and the corner of the Chapel, when he maneuvered around it, he was gone.

"Over here, who is it?" Gam shouted, still scanning the countryside for the mysterious green-eyed fellow.

"Where are you?" returned a young girl's voice. Gam waved, revealing himself but still looking this way and that, somewhat perplexed. He gazed at the approaching girl, dressed in Tinhallow robes.

"I arrived this morn and the Innkeeper was kind enough to tell me you would be here!" She exclaimed, breathlessly and striding forward with a purpose.

"Who the devil are ye child and why do ye look for this old windbag?" said Gam, giving up looking for Rake and subsequently diverting his full attention, if a quizzing one, upon the young girl.

"Why, I'm Loewen, your acolyte from Tinhallow!"

"Acolyte, girl, why, it's too many surprises for me!" guffawed Gam, "I was expecting someone with a little more height, a little more strength, and, dare I say, a little more balls!"

Gam realised he had gone a bit too far but he was still a little aggrieved that he had been interrupted just as he was about to throw this investigation wide open.

"I..I.." the girl composed herself. "Sorry to disappoint you but from what I understand from the Innkeep at your attempts to find this murderer, I dare say you need all the help you can get, balls or not!" she finished defiantly.

Gam stared after her for a moment, accepting the verbal slap gratefully, "splendid, good for ye, yes, good for ye!" he chuckled.

Loewen smiled back at Gam. She had been warned of his somewhat unruly and gruff ways for a friar – it appeared she would have to get used to this.

"Who was that?" she asked, indicating to the corner of the chapel where the green-eyed stranger had disappeared.

"Well my dear, that shady fella was probably Jonah's murderer and one of only two suspects that I..." he corrected himself, "...*we*, have. I believe his name is simply, Rake."

Loewen went silent and formed a big *O* with her lips.

"Indeed, my very same response when he approached me. Damned nerve if ye would. Clearly the days where the guilty *run* and the law *chase* are gone. Still." Gam wandered over to Loewen and gently grasped her wrist in greeting and engaged the young girl with a hearty shoulder slap.

"So young Loewen, welcome to Barrowdale - or Dead man's Scream to quote idle-mouths but perhaps somewhat more appropriate - I dare say ye will find this place as intriguing as I already have. Can I take it from your splendid riposte that ye know about the investigation?"

"Yes, yes I do."

"And have ye settled in to the Fool's Nook with baggage, belongings and supplies for the chapel?"

"Yes, yes I have." Loewen thought she should furnish further detail rather than appearing as a one word answering simpleton to her new mentor.

"Bardon kindly locked the chapel supplies in the store and he arranged for the mules to be watered and secured in the barn, next door." she smiled sweetly.

Loewen had seen near seventeen winters and was slight for her age which if anything made her look a little younger. There was nothing particularly noticeable about her appearance, except that perhaps she was a little drawn and Gam made a mental note to make sure that she filled out a bit with large plattered, invigorating meals whilst under his wing. She had a generous sprinkling of freckles across her features and an impish face that looked both cute and innocent, smiling from under shortly shawn and tussled hair. Her robe looked a little big.

Gam nodded, "Good, that will do just fine. So then Loewen, our prey seems to have scurried like the hare from the fox!" he exclaimed, deciding not to furnish the young acolyte with his reservations on Rake, just in case they were ill-founded.

"Do we give chase?" asked Loewen, looking excited.

"Well, I'm not sure where to start, Barrowdale is still quite a large body of land and my days of running this way and that are behind me!" chuckled Gam, patting his rotund belly. "Nope, he seems way too interested in us and our path, ye scared him off for now but I bet ye a barrel of fine ale Rake will be back to quiz and enquire, and, when he do, we'll be ready! I have a task for us to complete first. I found a drawing, scrawled by the old Jonah. Some kind of map, but to what, I cannot say. Nevertheless, I'm sure we will be enlightened once we uncover it and then, perhaps, we will start to solve some of this maddening conundrum. I dare say this Rake fellow would be damned interested in this map and if we can uncover the prize, we can use it to snare the vile murderer, may his bones rot!"

Loewen nodded enthusiastically.

"So be it young un, let us begin our quest." Gam unstoppered a wine skin and quenched his thirst. He then half-heartedly offered it to Loewen, who raised her hand to decline. Gam looked pleased and carefully stoppered it. He showed the young acolyte the old parchment.

"Just what does it mean?" she asked, glancing at it blankly.

"T' save me beating-around-the-shrubbery, I'll get to the chase of it. Before the fellow arrived, I searched through the chapel's collection of plans and charts of Barrowdale because it had occurred to me that the circles were in fact differing sized barrows!" Gam looked quite pleased with himself. "I over-laid a map, looking for some consistency, and, I found it. Tell me, did ye see a large rock on the way into Frostcross this morn Loewen? Large and proud on a hillock?

"Yes, on the brow overlooking the valley, near some old ruins?"

"Aye that is it - labelled as Scarpel Rock - and between it, and the Oakstone, is where we must go."

***

In the dark, cold chamber, undead stirred. Somewhere very near, vile and ancient necromantic enchantments seeped into the orifices of the corpse. The dark taint sought the decomposing brain and sparked a simple, evil, primordial command - to slay the living.

The creature stirred. Fingers flexed and broken finger-nails pulled the body along, gaining strength until it now stood in the darkness.

It was a member of the living dead, essentially not evil in life but intrinsically evil in undeath simply because of the very nature of it. In fact, in life, it had been a man. A simple sailor who enjoyed life's pleasantries but never had the taste for depravity and butchery unlike his old Captain. In trying to help his old Captain however - to re-kindle that relationship to how it was before he lost his eyelids - he had foolishly believed in him and subsequently died for it. Now he was no longer the man he was in life but an undead creature of primitive evil. A ghoulish creature that could feel the presence of the evil that had awakened it - tumbling over him in waves from somewhere behind the stone, barrow wall.

The hunger he now experienced pained him to his core and the lust for fresh meat was overwhelming and uncontrollable. Forcing his way out of a low, stone entranceway he hurried out into the darkness, the scent of young flesh sweeping over him from somewhere nearby. Gaining speed on butchered legs - held together only by the powerful necromantic enchantment buried in the barrow's wall - the undead abomination disappeared into the night. An abomination with a ravenous hunger.

***

Gam and Loewen had decided to follow the map via Frostcross to secure mounts. Gam saddled a horse, a big grey mare named Shadow, on loan from Gutiso's stables - even though Gutiso didn't know it yet - and Loewen chose a small brown pony. They were about to leave without word to the hook-nosed owner, when Gam had a nagging of the scruples - when he told Loewen, at first she thought he meant he had to visit the privy.

Gutiso's supply store was situated next to the Fool's Nook Inn, separated only by the stables and barn. The cream walls and green painted rails of Gutiso's Mercantile gleamed in the sun. A large, ornately painted sign swung overhead, proclaiming the establishment's name. Half a dozen hitching posts, each with two brass rings, fronted the store. A single wooden bench, also painted green, stood to the left of the door. The store's air of tidy prosperity contrasted sharply with the disrepair of the surrounding buildings. As Gam and Loewen approached, two young children jeered and taunted each other until one picked up a stone and threw it at the store window, but missed. The young, grubby faced scally was about to seize another missile when Gam caught up with him.

"Enough!" he roared, "leave it be pups, get along all of ye, or I'll..." Gam cuffed one child on the ears when he didn't flee fast enough to please him. They scurried away with Loewen sending a kick to their complacencies for good measure and smiled broadly for the satisfaction, if a little maliciously.

The fragrant smell of fresh-baked goods filled Gam's nose and he looked around keenly. The supply store was exactly that; every supply you could possibly want and some that you didn't know you wanted until you saw them and then desperately needed.

It was a two storey building crammed to the rafters with all things imaginable. Fantastical wares such as beautiful crafted compasses and rings lay casually beside common items, such as bits and bridles.

Gam watched Loewen meander to a counter at the back of the store. A flash of metal caught his attention. A shining but antiquated suit of armour stood near the windows, glowing with light from nearby lanterns. The windows were so covered with objects hanging up, that hardly any natural light shone through. Beside the armour, ran a counter that held new and used weapons, some with elaborate engravings. A well crafted mace rested behind glass, it's head formed in the shape of a face and the nose extended into a sharp spike. Adjacent to the counter was a stack of wooden stakes, several crocks containing water that was labelled *Blessed,* and several packs of silver bolts which were behind glass. Gam looked at the implements of undead slaying, puzzled - just hoping one would never need such things. He was inspecting a stake when Loewen called over, "Are those stakes? Don't you just chant or something?"

Gam guffawed, "some say that we clerics can weave divine power into powerful earth-shaking enchantments. Well let me tell ye, Hoppy-cock! I've been known to turn away some lesser undead and I'm one of the lucky ones, for some reason - that which I don't understand - my god grants me this gift.

Many of my Brothers from the Abbey can little as piss at a spirit than harm it with prayer - they may as well spit into the wind then take on undead!" Gam chuckled, continuing to examine the wares for sale whilst talking loudly to Loewen from one end of the store. "Now, the Father Superior - he's a different kettle of fish. Father-Superior Dodge is a ghost-layer of significant power – or an exorcist to ye.

I don't know if ye have heard this but there's an account where Dodge was called by a priest up north, whose parish was haunted by a phantom coach. Dodge and the priest - *Tills* I think his name - kept watch one night on the near moor, where it was usually seen. But it did not appear. Arranging to keep vigil another night, each turned homeward. At the bottom of a deep valley, Dodge's horse became uneasy, as if something was moving across the track in front of her. Defying her riders urging, she kept trying to turn around and finally Dodge threw the reins over her back and she started back over the moor. There, to his horror, Dodge saw the phantom coach, with Tills lying on the ground and the demon coachman standing over him. But, at the mere sight of Dodge closing in on him, the demon reportedly cried, 'Dodge is come! I must be gone!'"

Gam sniggered, "it sprang back on its coach, whereupon coach, horses and all vanished and did not return-"

The smell of baked bread suddenly grew stronger and Gam continued on following the scent. He turned at a large, old table, covered with bolts of fabric. Beyond the table, a pair of boots dangled from a post by their bootstraps. On a peg above the boots hung cloaks and small fishing nets. New tools, spare harness parts and saddles cluttered one corner as he walked on, still following the teasing aroma of bread.

Gam moved to the centre of the store, spying a large glass container, inside lay sugar creations. Gam licked his lips and rubbed his tummy. In an adjacent case Gam found a selection of fossils and precious stones, some bathed in rich colour, some chased in metal, others loose.

Soon Gam found the baked goods. Shelf after shelf brimmed with golden loaves. Gam saw current buns, loaves made of brown wheat and delicate pastries. Gam must have spent several mouth-watering moments eyeing up the pastries before *need* outweighed *politeness* and he pilfered a bun. He tucked into it like a boy with sweets.

Loewen groaned softly and planted a silver crown on the counter as payment for the tasty treat. She looked around impatiently.

"Look, he isn't here Gam, let us go."

Gam paused from his scoffing and glanced to the room beyond the counter, where he observed a wonderful arrangement of pipes and pots all mixing and separating unusually coloured ingredients. There was a brazier and several dozen alembic flasks, dishes, measuring devices and a set of scales. Gam tilted his head to indicate the scene to Loewen.

"Wonder what he's mixing back there," Gam offered and then under his breath, "I wonder if it's tasty?"

The two gave Gutiso a short while to return. When it was obvious he was not, they decided to leave the brewing alchemy and the store.

"We'll arrange payment later." said Gam offering a jovial salute to the sign and sauntered up to their new mounts like a sailor on the dock.

They took the cart-track east out of Frostcross and one not often travelled. The track ran alongside stone cow sheds, some in reasonable order, others not. Soon the track petered out into a footpath where the long brush to the side of the track now thinned out to a meadow, with moss and grass covered rock outcrops.

After several hours, at the point where they met a stream, the path seemed to stop and become nothing more than a faint animal trail running through the scrub. The stream was shallow but furious in its bubbling decent. It narrowed suddenly and rushed over a pebble and rocky bed. Their horses however, easily traversed the stream and continued up the opposite bank. In the distance Gam could begin to make out the brown barrow lands, coloured that way by the low lying heather and gorse that covered the region.

Gam noticed great furrows in the land as they rode on. Water had long since gone from the gorse covered earthworks, so that now just the wind channelled through the furrows creating low groans and moans, and Gam instinctively held his reins tighter and closer to his chest.

The earthworks led them to the wide expanse of burial mounds, collapsed and intact chambered cairns. Gam and Loewen pulled out of the heather and gorse before the great Scarpel Rock. With harness jingling softly on the breeze, they turned their mounts to the east and the clouds shifted, drifted and sunlight shone through, bathing the scene. The beautiful brilliance picked out the deep colours of the heather and gorse but then the golden orb disappeared as fast as it had arrived, casting the area in a grey dreariness once again. The picture perfect scene, brief though it was, did seek to lift the companions spirits as they calmly looked up at the Oakstone as it stood watchful, guarding its secrets. It stood to attention surveying over the barrows like a guardian and likewise the huge and high set Scarpel Rock appeared on their left. This part of Barrowdale was strewn with old weathered and ragged tors and ancient monuments left by a people long since lost to history. Some stood close to each other, set in circular and horse shoe patterns, whilst others stood alone atop grass reclaimed knolls - like outcasts from a group.

Gam's experiences with visiting barrows were not particularly pleasant ones and the prospect of doing so again was not appealing. The idea of entering some great and long-dead chieftain's final resting place did not sit well with him. Obviously there was the mark of disrespect but defiling and disturbing a sacred burial chamber unnerved him. Gam had fought the walking dead on occasions, he could still remember the first time as a young acolyte emptying the contents of his stomach at the sight of a shambling zombie. It wouldn't have been too bad in the eyes of his peers and companions except that on the following three occasions his supper had followed the same route. Gam shook his head and shuddered. No, the idea still repulsed him and he swallowed hard - the prospect of facing more minions of undeath in such a place as this was not lost on him. He uncorked his wine skin and took a long bracing swig of strong mead, re-stoppered the skin and belched respectfully. That seemed to have settled his stomach for now.

Setting his mind to things other than shuffling skin suites, he took out the parchment from his robe and examined the map scrawled upon it. Loewen stood high in her stirrups, surveying the barrow field and trying to glance over Gam's shoulder. He quickly re-folded and placed the map back to its snug resting place. He nodded over to a long and somewhat imposing barrow situated slightly further away beyond an area of low gorse, exactly as the map suggested. It was surrounded by smaller rocks compounded over the ages and could just make out a slab of stone at its highest point, presumably the roof of the central chamber he surmised. "I believe this is it!" he announced.

Loewen slid out of her saddle and quickly made her way around the chambered cairn clutching a large lantern. Gam was glad for her keenness and she didn't therefore witness him half dismount, half fall, off his horse. He quickly straightened his robe, patting the muzzle of his horse - winking at it's dark twinkling eyes and lifted the pack to his back.

"It's big!" exclaimed Loewen.

"Aye," replied Gam, catching up with his young aid, picking a path through the thick gorse, "must be near fifty feet long - someone of importance I reckon."

Soon they found a black opening in the cairn where long ago someone had excavated its opening. The entrance had collapsed slightly and the lintel stone was now resting cock-eyed and at waist height. Gam grimaced and studied the moss covered rocks and glanced down to his somewhat portly girth, sighing. He took another cheeky swig of mead, only to be caught and met with stern eyes from Loewen. "Look, I gave my life to my god and sacrificed all, even mi lord wouldn't deny me this small pleasure under such circumstances!"

Slate grey clouds began to loom overhead and the wind picked up, howling through the gorse and long grass. Gam and Loewen stood in silence taking in the scene. Loewen was keen to explore but Gam shivered softly, he new only to well what they could face inside. He led the way none the less, gently pushing the girl behind him, "Look, I ain't gonna be responsible if you fall down some crippling trap or have your hair ripped out by some spectre, right!"

He crouched down and entered, Loewen closely following and peering passed him. A stale air clung to the walls like mist and Gam hesitated, letting his eyes adjust to the gloom. The stone lintel was larger than he thought and ran some way, supporting the entire ceiling of the entry chamber. With a frown etched on his face he felt the floor, rubbing stone and dirt between forefinger and thumb, "looks like something has made this area damp." Gam indicated for Loewen to pass him the lantern and lit the candle within with flint and striker. Raising it above his head Gam probed in further toward a narrow passage, straight ahead. He reached the black maw and let the lantern's light illuminate as far as he could before stepping in. He half looked and half felt with his feet at a few stairs going down and when he reached the bottom he was able to stand fully erect. He couldn't hear the wind at all now and it was eerily quiet, Loewen's breathing and his own rasping was suddenly very apparent. The smell was still of staleness but as he moved slowly and cautiously down the passage a new smell offended his nose - like rotting meat. He reassuring tapped his hammer swinging at his side and approached another chamber where he let the candles light do its job. The chamber was quite large and roofed with massive stone blocks; the space between was packed with small stones, a kind of dry walling he surmised, it also had two passages to his left and right.

"This must be the burial chamber - it's quite intact - and there are two passages running from it, probably an artifact chamber that would hold relics for use in an after-life and the other possibly leading to another burial chamber." Gam relayed to Loewen as she glanced in under his arm.

"What is that smell?" she asked, wrinkling her nose.

"The smell of the dead" intoned Gam, glancing to the far corners of the chamber.

"Surely there would be no smell after all these hundreds, if not thousands of seasons? It smells like a butcher's shop. And whoever was buried here has been carried away by tomb robber's ages ago - I expect along with any burial artifacts!"

"You are indeed correct young-un, this smell is from something else, something recent, something still... sticky!" the word caught in Gam's throat.

"Look," he said, indicating a stone slab propped to one side. The tough rock had been cut and shaped with basic implements. "The original burial would have been under that, probably in furs and though there is nothing now, do you see the reflection from the candle, something shining?"

Loewen nodded.

"That's blood, and fresh." Gam moved forward and let the hammer swing freely into his waiting hand, "here, take this." He passed the lantern to Loewen who stepped in but hugged the stone wall.

Gam stepped down into the burial pit and the sickening stench was far stronger. He held his breath as long as he could whilst he inspected the area.

"A body has been here, leaking and lying here recent. Where it is now I don't know, but we better search the other chambers to be sure!"

"Who could it have been?" asked Loewen, her eyes wide in the lantern light. "Is this what the map led to - a body?"

Gam shook his head in thought. It was not what he was expecting - he coveted a neatly written tome providing answers to all his burning questions. Although he realistically knew it could be nothing so profound, he had expected, dared hope even, that it was something more obvious and tactile rather than just the deposits from a corpse. "I reckon this Rake fella!" Gam suddenly exploded, "he nay impatient to see what we find - to succeed where he failed - there must be something here! Let us keep looking."

The two passages were much narrower than the passage-grave. The walls were finely packed stone while the roof was corbelled and each led to a rounded or polygonal chamber where areas were broken up into segments by low cross stone slabs and pairs of stones projecting from the walls. Nothing had been left by tomb-robbers and treasure seekers bar a few small bits of crumbling bone.

The two companions decided to search them thoroughly; Gam took the slightly larger chamber whilst Loewen lit another candle and took the smaller tomb.

Gam pressed himself into the first section, shining the lantern in all corners. He felt along the stone, looking for any hidden compartments. By the time he reached the forth and penultimate section he was beginning to ache from the stooping and took to half-heartedly pushing at the stone, his feelings sinking. As he did so, a squeal almost made him jump.

"Loewen, what is it? Are ye alright?" Gam paused and set himself in case he had to rush to her rescue. Silence met his ears. He was just about to hurry to the adjacent chamber when Loewen returned his questioning hail.

"I'm fine thanks Gam, t'was a big spider is all!" Gam shook his head, he had thought she had found something, her squeal had certainly sounded delightful! 'Fool girl,' he sighed, "bloomin' spiders would ye? Stop fannying around." He moved onto the last section and searched the stone within, but to no avail.

They withdrew from the chambers and the barrow completely, glad to breathe fresh air again but a little dismayed by the lack of a discovery, and, to add insult to injury, a fine rain had begun to fall.

Heading back to the Inn Gam was lost to his thoughts. Loewen was likewise very quiet and Gam just assumed she shared his disenchantment.

The two companions stalked wearily into the Fool's Nook Inn. The inviting warmth and prospect of a good hearty meal cheered them as they entered, the fire glow illuminating their wind-burnt faces.

They were quite damp from the rain and had spent longer out in it due to Gam spotting the dwarf, Grim, observing them. He had taken after the dwarf, determined to turn their afternoon into a positive one but alas had failed to catch him and lost him in the descending mists. Loewen had learnt there and then that this was Gam's second and last suspect and consequently, he had befallen even more to frustration.

She, on the other hand, had just simply yearned to return to the Inn.

The majority of the patrons were seated on wooden benches and old chairs, some were standing and encircling Bardon who looked quite comfortable in a larger, cushioned, winged-back chair. Gam recognised Gutiso who was seated at his usual table, looking as miserable as ever. He also spied Thesden, Tith and Ervan. Lanterns illuminated the rafters of the Inn, whilst the crackles and pops from the cheerfully burning fire mingled with Bardon's baritone voice as he told his tale.

Outside, the strong ocean wind whipped sleet through the black trees and a strong rain began to lash against the slate roof. Whereas inside, it was a refuge of tranquility, patrons listened intently and leaned in close to Bardon. They wetted their throats with great gulps of ale from fast replenishing wenches as the large Innkeeper lit his long pipe and recounted his yarn, just like every seasonal fifth night in Frostcross.

Gam quietly sat on a bar stool and indicated to a serving girl who came over with a tray of foam-brimming ale and a platter. Gam gratefully received the wooden board laden with finest Calil cheese, a freshly baked half-loaf that was still warm, pickled onions and eggs, delicate silver-fish of the Sea of Gold Lightning and a brimming tankard of Barley wine. Smiling at the delicious variety he took a crisp bite out of a large pickled onion and guzzled back the robust draught. The flavours were hearty and gratifying, and with it, Gam's smile grew broader. Good simple food, far better than any culinary Chandor ponciness.

Loewen settled down next to him on the taproom floor, her legs drawn up under her arms and chin.

"The shockin' news was received in this very here Inn," said Bardon with gusto and blowing leaf-smoke up toward the rafters, "Barrowdale had been invaded again, an ambitious foreigner, with an eye for plunder and conquest. Captain Bulwyf the Giant, known as the Sand Waster - for no settlement was left standin' after a raid by his vicious cut-throat pirates!

Bulwyf had landed by long boats up at Rona Rea and traveled south down Barrowdale's coast. He had unfurled his black banner, proclaimin' his dastardly self and intent.

Whilst Captain Bulwyf brushed aside small camps of our local opposition - like the woodsmen from Bracken - Father Ardd reacted with haste, summoning men to arms with long peels of the Chapel bell. They marched north from Frostcross to the river and east following the coast's meanderin' route, hopin' to cut Bulwyf and his pirates off before they reached Frostcross.

Father Ardd reached the river on the second night after Captain Bulwyf's ship, the Night Star, had been originally spotted off the coast. There he learned from his woodsmen scouts that the pirates had no idea his force was comin' and believed them to be still cowering behind their doors. Indeed Bulwyf and his retinue were expecting to arrogantly strike into Frostcross unhindered. Ardd resolved to launch his force - the Fellows of Frostcross - consistin' of farmers, woodsmen and a small contingent of mercenaries, against the pirates the next morn.

It was sunny and reports say the small force was all very cheerful. The unsuspectin' invaders ambled onwards to the river. Ardd led his force straight toward a bridge, fully armed and motivated for battle against their foe. Here was another chance to drive the hated sea-thieves from Barrowdale again!

The pirates crossed the bridge and those with the keenest eyes spotted a small cloud of dust on a trail from the north. At the base of the cloud the pirates saw what looked like the glint of sunlight on broken ice. It was the weapon tips of the approaching Dalesmen, with Father Ardd at their head.

The rabble pirates were spread out on both sides of the river connected only by the small bridge. Ardd had sent a small force of woodsmen archers and they approached from the west, trapping those on the north bank in a bottle neck. Some scrambled to get back across the bridge, while others stood and fought against overwhelming odds. Bulwyf and his first mate argued. Should they retreat, back north, or stand and fight? Kidd, his number one, guessed that the Dalesmen would be near invincible in a fight for their homeland with the surprised, unprepared and disorganised pirates. He begged the Captain to retreat and organise resistance but Bulwyf the Giant had never run from a battle. He ordered his black banner to be unfurled and commented grimly that, although he would doubtless be killed, he would give the Dalesmen one hell of a poundin'. So with that, the pirate Captain lifted his hefty cutlass, pushed passed his fleeing men toward the bridge, reacting as a hero worthy of eternal flame.

After the Dalesmen had scythed through his panic-stricken men on the north bank of the river, the giant Bulwyf stood astride the bridge and held up the entire Barrowdale force, gaining his men precious time to re-group behind. With his vicious sword he hewed nine Dalesmen as they tried to rush the bridge. Under his black, fluttering banner of death, Bulwyf defended his thieving kin, sneering and growling at the Dalesmen with contempt. It was only after one of the enterprising swords-for-hire swam beneath the bridge and stabbed upwards with a spear between the wooden slats of the bridge right into Bulwyf's unprotected groin and exposed legs, did the pirate fall.

It is said that Ardd was greatly annoyed with the mercenary for his ungallant move and dismissed him from service. Ardd would 'ave challenged Bulwyf to honourable single combat on the bridge in order to save lives. However, as the Dalesmen burst across the bridge, the pirates hurriedly locked themselves and their few small shields together in a wall. The Dalesmen called for the pirates to surrender, expectin' compliance after the death of their captain, but surprisingly it had only heightened the pirate's determination after witnessin' such unusual heroism and self-sacrifice from their leader. The pirate now in command – Kidd - shouted back foul words of abuse, statin' that the pirates would succeed in taking Frostcross for their own. To this, Ardd replied the best they could hope for was 'seven feet of Frostcross soil in which to be buried in!'"

The Inn's patrons cheered a rousing chorus, before letting Bardon continue, "with that, Ardd led the charge toward the pirate shield wall."

Gam was suddenly aware of the huge task he had undertaken here in this isolated region and the leadership that the people would look to him for. Initially it made his stomach drop, the thought of not living up to his new duties and responsibilities in this community - not to mention his heroic predecessor - made him feel a little dizzy. However, after the initial pang of illness had subsided it left him with a swell of pride. Here, he could make a difference. Here, he would be wanted. He re-focused on Bardon's yarn, smiling with a new sense of resolve.

"As the two sides clashed, Dalesmen steel caused carnage among the pirate ranks. Kidd left the protection of his fellows and charged ferociously at Ardd with a sword in each hand. A furious fight ensued until Kidd was killed, receivin' a mace to the face. His body was dragged back behind the pirate wall and again Ardd offered terms, but the pirates shouted back that they would rather fall in battle than accept mercy from a landlubber. The pirates were a stubborn enemy to be sure.

The battle was hard fought but in time the pirate line began to fragment. A small group of pillagin' pirate infiltrators had heard the commotion of battle and joined as reinforcements but they were too late, by the time they arrived all they could do was sacrifice themselves for a cause already lost. The pirate host was slaughtered, their leadership destroyed.

The bridge was also near destroyed in the fightin' and has never been re-built, it was situated almost at the point where the Ferrymen operate nowadays.

After the victory, our noble Father Ardd showed mercy and allowed a very young pirate banner-bearer called Jonah, to take Captain Bulwyf's body back to the Night Star and set off immediately and nay to ever return." Bardon finished, slugging back strong, chilled mead. "And that was the last pirate incursion into our fair dale - was in my pappy's time, when I was a wee sprog."

"And long may it remain the last!" cheered Tith, slapping her thigh which was barely squeezed into soft, leather breeches that accentuated her curvy figure. The crowd raised their drinks in agreement.

"Maybe not *live* pirates," muttered Gutiso, throwing Gam a look of disdain, "plenty-a Sea-Spectres though."

Bardon raised his eyes and the crowd went as silent as a snowfall. After a moment longer they went back to chatting amongst themselves, overlooking the Alchemist's pessimistic mind-set. At that moment Gam realised he hadn't compensated Gutiso for the use of the horses and wondered if he had missed them. Judging by the look of disgust still fixed upon him, he reckoned so. He quickly looked the other way and then realised that Loewen was missing and must have already gone to bed, although he had not observed her slip away.

Gam was about to slip up to his room when Tith propped herself at the counter next to him, smiling, she ordered two drinks. Ice-cold mead - served this way because that is how they came. Then following on briskly, served straight up at room temperature, because that was the way Gam preferred them and then in a 2:1 ratio of whiskey and mead, because that was how Tith preferred them. Gam finished with a cheeky ale chaser. And then he fell up the stairs.

***

"Is it safe to be goin' out so late, pa?" asked the young boy as he jogged behind his father, attempting to keep up with the adult's large strides.

"I told yer Kiav, we won't be long! I 'ave a little bit of business to take care of and then we'll be back, as quick as you can say I wanna-pot-o'-gold! Alright?"

"Alright, pa." Kiav replied, not wanting to antagonise his father. He knew only too well what one received when you antagonised Edomal the Aggravator - his father, and a somewhat unknown ruffian and smuggler of Frostcross. Kiav subconsciously rubbed his back from the beating he had received yester eve. The boy looked up at the night sky, searching for the big moon he knew was up there somewhere. He felt a particular connection with the glowing orb that watched over Barrowdale. Whenever he was thrown into his room after a *discipline lesson* - or at least that is what his father would call the beatings - he would stare out of his little window in the attic, talking to that patient sphere and sharing his childhood thoughts. Kiav had little choice, he was allowed no friends.

Silently he padded behind his father as they cleared the ramshackle buildings and mish-mash of shelters that were the outskirts of Frostcross. Edomal and Kiav lived in a small and shabby stone building on Rotten Row, somehow Edomal had swindled his way into occupancy. The boy was not as stupid as his father thought him. Having no friends and forced to run errands for his father and accompany him on slave smuggling jobs for pirates in the middle of the night - where Kiav's slight frame was of benefit to squeeze into certain places - he had heard and witnessed a great deal. Much more than any other boy of his own age would have or should have. And with Kiav he watched and remembered everything. Watching his father as he brutally went about his business, learning to hate him, learning to hate the pirates.

The nights were long in this season and it took quite a while for the two to weave their way to the coast. But soon, under Kiav's comforting glowing moon above, the two figures drew close. High overhead a storm began to brew in the night sky and rain clouds blew inland. "So, where we goin' then, pa?"

"Stop askin' bleedin' questions you pup! I'm tryin t' concentrate..." Edomal stopped in the middle of the stony track where it forked left and right, examining an overly large and clearly drawn map of the area. Kiav silently guided his father over to the side of the trail, gaining the cover of the hedge rather then the exposed openness of the track. Kiav often wondered how his father survived this dangerous line of business with such an unaware attitude and perhaps a little jealously worked its way into his beatings.

"Oi! Kiav. Look 'ere. Any idea how to read this bloody map?" said Edomal through gritted teeth, pawing at the map.

Kiav did not fancy a beating tonight. "Well pa, if you can't read it, I sure as 'ell can't," Kiav lied, "though you did say earlier that the cliff was a-that way!" he finished, pointing ahead toward the right fork.

"Y..Yess, um, that's right. I did say that, didn't I?" Edomal stuttered, accepting the boy's blatant lie as obvious truth. "Now quit your dallying Kiav and follow me!"

"Yes dad," Kiav offered for effect, "So. Why are we heading to the cliffs?"

Edomal nearly stopped dead at Kiav's probing, "very well boy. We are goin' to signal a ship and take delivery of the gold I was promised!" Edomal smirked and rubbed his hands in anticipation of gold, like a true pirate. His expression was one that implied Kiav would see none, as always.

As Edomal prepared the lantern a deep groan from behind startled the father and son as they looked out to the roaring waves. It was a godforsaken noise that brought the hair on the back of the boy's neck to attention and spread goose bumps across his skin. Whatever this was it had caused Edomal to stop and take a worried look back. He cast a nervous glance to his son and then back to the edge of the cliff.

"What in the name of the devils-hairy-crotch was that?" whispered Edomal.

Kiav could not reply, a cold fear had rooted him to the spot. All he could do was stare into the darkness ahead. Edomal kicked at the boy, indicating for him to go and check. When Kiav did not respond he took out a small cudgel from inside his cloak and wielded it threateningly at the boy. A small tear brimmed in Kiav's eye as the shock of the situation sank in. Either disappoint his father and face another beating or walk into the face of some unknown horror that may lurk behind. A young boy's imagination could create some sinister creatures that made fearful moaning noises like this - and the picture forming in his head at the moment was no exception.

"Father, please, I..." with a deep, hollow sounding thud, the cudgel

struck across Kiav's back, making him wince and dislodge the tear.

"Move, you damnable baby!" cursed Edomal, bringing the cudgel down again on his son's back. Further tears rolled, but Kiav was not moving. The boy dropped to his knees, attempting to shield his body from his father's strikes. After several more clouts he curled down into a tight ball, whimpering in fear and pain.

"Why you..." Edomal began, lifting the cudgel high. His pause in the *lesson* was caused by a flash of movement, just a five-pace away. Edomal opened his mouth to scream, but excruciating pain filled his head. He dropped the cudgel instantly and lost control over his arms and legs, dropping to the ground with no more dignity than a sack of potatoes. Something moved, twisting an incredible pain through his head. His vision began to blur until his surroundings went out of focus completely. The overwhelming pain caused his mouth to blubber uncontrollably but still no sound came forth.

Kiav sensed a presence, not dissimilar to how he felt when awoken at night, under the cover of his patchwork quilt and certain he was not alone, and with an eerie prickling sensation sweeping over his body dared not look up to confirm it. A deep thump of vibration rocked through him as he felt what could only be his father's body falling to the ground, followed by a wet slurping sound. Kiav, just as he had done on those times in the middle of the night, still did not dare look up from his huddled position.

Paralysis held Edomal. He could not move, breathe or scream. A horrific sucking sensation echoed within his head. He gazed at the huddled figure of his son, not three feet away, but with all the strength he could muster he could not cry out for help. Pain wove its way through his head again. Something broke and snapped, somewhere deep, momentarily granting a release from the terrible pressure in his head. Cold horror replaced the ebbing pain as Edomal's eyes could just about make out the feet of a figure. With dire fear of the worst kind Edomal glanced his eyes up to the figure's face.

The gruesome visage that met him offered no comfort - a twisted, sickening display of undeath. Bits of skin hung from the white bone structure of the things face, the muscle and tendons underneath popped with foul puss, which ebbed down the creature's rag-tag front. Dark red liquid escaped from between sharp teeth and those round, lidless staring eyes...

It dived down toward Edomal's paralysed form. The twin rows of dagger-like teeth crunched down together with eager anticipation at the bloodied mess that was Edomal. It was now obvious that somehow the thing had surprised Edomal from behind and had bitten through his head with its enlarged jaw. Still paralysed and unable to raise his arms in defence, Edomal watched in terror as the rows of sharp teeth bit into his face - so that one of his eyes was staring down the things gullet. Unable to respond, he felt himself being thrown around like some rag doll, at the mercy of the ghoulish abomination. Edomal felt a rushing sensation flush his cheeks as he knew, with morbid realisation, the creature was feeding on the blood gushing from his head wound.

With disgust Edomal willed himself to move. He knew he would fail, but he had to try. As thunder rumbled high above and the rain began to fall, he failed.

The thing disengaged from his face, letting his own blood blind his remaining working eye. His body flexed in revulsion as the thing rammed its hand into his mouth, forcing his teeth inward and snapping them. With successive thrusts the thing forced its way to the back of Edomal's throat and down. With gasping, choking fits and rippling spasms jerking his body, Edomal, at last, fell unconscious.

Not three feet away the huddled, whimpering form of his son dared not move.

***

Gam's room at the Fool's Nook Inn was spacious, the expanse of cream plaster walls broken only by paintings of the surrounding countryside and views from the Shoremeet. The ceiling timbers were white-washed and decorated with painted garlands of flowers. The cot had a thick comfortable mattress and Gam was pleasantly surprised to find soft sheets.

The windows had stained glass sections imitating the sea, rimmed with lead. They opened out over the entrance of the Inn and half-overlooking Gutiso's store and stable.

Gam took off his robe haphazardly, threw on a white night-shirt and filled a china bowl with water from an old jug, splashing his face. Feeling more refreshed and somewhat stable now after his ripping drinking session, he slipped on a night hat - complete with small bobble end - and slipped into the cot. Stretching his toes he listened to the storm brewing outside and wondered how quickly he could jump from the cot, shut the window and get back to his comfy retreat. The decision was a difficult one and had now well and truly taken precedence over his thoughts on the days events. Somewhere in the decision making process he began to doze as the storm raged outside and battered the simple windows.

A flash of lightning startled him awake and he pulled the blanket up in reflex. He shuffled over onto his side and counted the number of times a door somewhere nearby banged in the wind as he tried to fall asleep. Thirty seven, to his reckoning.

Lightning momentarily lit the room again and almost instantly the thunderclap followed. Gam awoke and bolted upright, clearly he was feeling edgy and wondered how long he had been asleep. The first thought that popped into his mind, grudgingly and under protest, was the chambered tomb. The second, was that he just somehow must have missed something there - his very being cried out with the fact. He had been trying to push it from his mind, with little success. Why didn't he just accept it? Why didn't he face it?

He thought of Bardon's account of Father Ardd's exploits and the feeling of pride returned. There and then he decided he would go back to the barrow, forgetting his reservations, and, if necessary, turn it upside down in his search. Discovering what Jonah's map led to was his only chance of gaining the upper hand and hopefully some level of understanding. If that didn't work he would just have to track down this Rake fellow blindly.

Wiping his eyes, he gave into the storm and padded across to the window and shut it. He wiped clear the bottom two windowpanes, casually observing the lane below and spied the banging side door to Gutiso's barn. The occasional Dalesman hurried passed trying their best to shelter from the driving rain and not to slip in the quagmire of cack. Gam was just about to mock-dive into the cot when another noise made his ears prick. It was another bang, but a door somewhere nearby, in fact from the very next room - Loewen's room. He would have expected the young acolyte to be fast asleep by now and wondered if all was well. Perhaps the storm was bothering her? Struggling, he nearly dived into the soft warmth once again before his conscience got the better of him and decided he should probably go and check on her.

Gam unlocked his door with a turn of the key and strolled towards Loewens'. He grimaced, a splinter from the rough floorboards had lovingly found his foot. How kind, he thought, screwing his face up with the pain and muffling a curse with his hand as he hobbled up to the room. Giving a gentle rap on the door and not thinking of a young girl's need for privacy, opened it. He remembered too late that he should have awaited a verbal offer before marching in just as he spied Loewen half-diving, half-naked, into her cot in obvious fright. He mumbled an embarrassed apology and only snuck quick peeks from behind the door to make sure she had her covers up.

"Sorry to catch ye a little *nekkid*-" Gam stopped, quickly changing subject from Loewen's state of undress, "be ye alright young-un? I heard a noise and wondered if the storm weighed on your mind?"

"I..I'm fine, thank you Gam. You just startled me is all, and yes, the storm doesn't help!"

"Indeed, I.." Gam then paused as he noted from his stolen glances behind the door that her hair was quite wet. "Your hair is wet?" he remarked, for lack of a more subtle question, also noting the large size of her room compared to his paltry space. He made a mental note to speak with Bardon. Sitting in the corner was her pack and small chest - which remained unpacked - and several of her outer garments were dispersed across the room. He noticed a short bow sticking out from the top of her pack.

"Yes, Bardon kindly supplied me with some hot water and hot milk in fact. I thought a bath might help me relax, to be honest Gam, that barrow was quite spooky." The look that Loewen offered was one of complete innocence and initially Gam felt a little ashamed that he had taken the girl into a horrid tomb with little thought to her feelings. He had not considered that.

"I'm sorry to hear that but glad you're being sensible. I'm only the next door if ye need me lass. Take care and try and get some sleep." Gam offered a warm smile and quietly shut the door. As the door met the frame he heard Loewen offer her thanks. He stood staring at the door for a ten-breath and then returned silently to his room. He hoped there were no spiders lurking in her room, remembering the incident in the barrow.

"Sweet girl," he offered out loud. "So why do I feel like sheep's wool has challenged mi eyes of late?"

Gam settled back into bed and as the thunder rumbled and the rain petered against the glass, the door banged one hundred and sixty-eight times before he finally fell asleep this time.

***

Gam found himself standing and staring at a simple, primitive stone structure which sat humbly on the plains that he realised by the distant mountain range would later become known as *Barrowdale* - standing blankly in this seemingly prehistoric country, a black silhouette against the evening light.

Several men, women and a handful of children lifted one of the final chisel-shaped stones into position adjacent to the lintel-stone above the entrance of the stone structure. Turfs had been recently laid on top of the stones forming the crude but safe and camouflaged chamber. Gam silently observed the family as they finished and stood back, unaware of his presence and ostensibly, very proud of their unsullied dwelling.

One of the larger men - probably the leader - rubbed his arm across his high stepped forehead, characteristic of a primitive race and placed a calloused hand on the shoulder of his mate. She looked to him and smiled offering a gentle grunt of satisfaction and adjusted her crudely stitched animal hides that kept her warm from the biting, evening winds gusting across the plains from the sea. A nearby trail across the plain was dry and rough - a scar across the land.

In the distance, Gam suddenly observed five men looming on large, horned mammoths set against the horizon. Somehow he felt that these were intruders and although he could not apparently communicate, he instinctively let out a warning.

The Leader of this small family group, apparently named as of the sound *Raa,* saw them from the entrance.

He beckoned to a nearby male, who appeared to be a brother judging by his similar squinting dark eyes, bushy eye brows and long hair-line.

"Raa", he spoke, "Raa", and pointed to the mammoth on the horizon, as he saw the dust rising in the distance from the great beast's passage.

His brother thumped his chest and intoned "Sheg" - presumably *his* name. The thumping of his chest indicating danger and defiance. Raa nodded in return and motioned to his female mate for a huge spear leaning against the stone. She hurriedly moved to pass the ash shaft with its leather fixed flint end.

Raa and Sheg watched the mammoth disappear behind a line of trees. Then they stopped looking. They entered the stone chamber where the remaining men, females and children were preparing for the night in front of a recently and hurriedly prepared fire at its centre.

Gam, keeping quiet - though it did not seem to matter - padded in behind as Raa placed his hands on his two daughter's heads and gently guided them toward the corner. He pointed at his son - somewhat older than his daughters - and indicated the rack where their spears rested. The boy nodded and moved towards the weapons. The other men took note from the boy and followed, noting Raa's furrowed brow they grunted nervously. The women stopped at that sound, realisation sweeping over their thick features.

At a crossroads on the trail, at a point where a stream met the trail, the mammoth and its riders did not turn from the main trail but continued toward the stone structure.

Now, just a small distance away, the men traveled in silence. Wickedness marred their features – masks of cold dispassion and malice. They were similar in appearance to those they sought, but their eyes were mere pin-pricks of blackness – black as coal, and their skin was greyer in hue – they came from the northern desert, they came with hatred…

The man, Raa, pressed his lips against his daughter's foreheads and tussled their long and matted hair. A forlorn murmur escaped from his lips and with sad eyes he pointed toward the earthen chamber floor. Instinctively, the girls searched their father's eyes for something that might help them understand. They saw nothing.

Their father leaned over and kissed them again.

The brother lifted a large wooden plank, revealing a dark hole in the earth. The girls let themselves fall into the hole. The earth was hard and smelt vaguely of ash. One of the women snatched at a fur and let it down to the girls who took it to lie upon. They spread it on the bottom of the small pit and laid down.

They heard a commotion from above - one of their uncles, and the sound of urgent shouting. They watched as their brother lowered the plank back into place and observed an overwhelming sadness in his eyes. Then it all went black. But their brother's eyes stayed fixed in their simple minds. They heard furs pulled over the plank and the motes of light piercing its edges disappeared. They heard their father grunting, followed by sounds of agreement from the others of the family.

The girls were lying on their sides, knees drawn up to their chests, curled up, safe. We are happy here, they tried to convince themselves. They held each other in the dark and hardly dared to breathe. They new what they had to do. They had to be silent.

The silence was broken by war-like shouting - from somewhere outside, then the fearsome roar of a mammoth. Calls of defiance and anger rose up from above them, from their family. The girls flattened themselves. They felt the earth, felt safe by it. The earth would not betray them - but offer protection like it did to the small furry animals of the plains they used to watch running into their burrows to escape the hunters. This day *they* were those animals.

They heard further commotion and then a scream - their mother! And their eyes startled open with shock. It went silent for a two-breath and then came a terrific scream that was cut off as sudden as it had begun. The two girls hugged each other, trembling slightly. They guessed that their father and uncles would be throwing spears, then there was another scream - a death wail, but they didn't recognise the voice. It was followed by a dull thud as ash staff met unknown staff and the noise and commotion was all around them. The plank vibrated as feet danced across it engaged in a terrific struggle. There was further shouting, a call of surprise, a loud crash and silence again.

Suddenly the light came streaming into the hole and they threw their arms up to shield themselves from whatever had discovered them. It was their brother.

He had a cut over one eye and his spear was broken. He lifted his sisters up and steered them away from the hole and the broken bodies of their uncle and aunt laying grotesquely at the rear of the stone chamber.

As they moved toward the opening and the commotion of fighting outside, a grey-skin burst into the chamber and stopped abruptly at spotting the children. The four stood motionless, staring at each other.

They heard the hoarse voice of their father, shouting as he struggled with a grey-skin attacker, knowing that one of this fell brute's kin had slipped in after his children.

The boy pushed his sisters behind him and held up his broken spear. The reaching flames reflected evilly in the man's eyes as he observed the children murderously. He smiled, as the licking flames crackled fiercely as the wind reached inside the chamber. He smiled wider, in knowing anticipation - about to strike.

The boy knew much of life even at his young age and reacted before the grey-skin and launched his spear. But into emptiness.

The grey-skin responded instinctively and threw his spear. The force lifted the child up off the ground and hurled him at the stone wall in a mess of blood like a bird plucked from the sky by an arrow.

The sisters threw themselves at the ground. For a moment the two girls looked at each other. Then from the eldest throat came a dull, horrible howl. The youngest trembled uncontrollably - she could only stare at her brother's body, lying in his own blood, his mouth hideously wide.

The eldest sister quickly quietened to silence but the silence frightened her more. The stone chamber - their new home, stank of calamity and she wanted to flee from the vile scene.

It was then that their father entered, his flint axe smeared crimson, he ignored his fallen son, he could not have faced the pain in this moment of crisis.

Shouting came from outside - more grey-skins approached.

He stared at two pairs of motionless, staring eyes and then his eldest daughter blinked and raised her head higher to look at him. He studied her for a two-breath, eyes, lips, hair. Then he held out his hands toward them both and pulled them up and away out into the night. He offered to them a small jet-black statuette. They recognised it immediately as the cherished artifact their father prized. It was of a roughly-sculptured torso with only the beginning of stumps where the arms, legs and neck would be. The children had always shied away from its unnatural design and when the daughters touched it they began to feel ill. Surely these grey-skins couldn't be after this? Could they?

Their father then pushed them into an urgent run and they almost stumbled. He growled menacingly as the remaining three grey-skins took up the pursuit. To cover his daughters escape the father turned to meet the attackers head on and drew a large flint axe from the leathers at his waist and began to spin the staff threateningly in his other hand.

The girls watched for an instant and then took flight as their father had bid them.

Flee. Flee. Keep running. The uneven ground flashed passed their eyes.

Flee. Flee. Keep running, like the small animals do.

Flee. Flee. The night time silence was broken by a morose howl from the distant hills – other predators were stalking the plains this night.

Flee. Flee. Keep running, flee for the hills.

Gam found himself following after the girls, when the attack had come he had tried to intervene, but to no avail, he was unable to effect his surroundings, unable to make them see him. All he could do was follow and hope.

After sometime of harried running, he discerned a cave mouth under a lone peak looming up out of the gloom. From his knowledge of Barrowdale - such as that was - he was sure it was what the locals called Iron Peak.

The cave was like a jagged, black claw, protruding from the land. But the darkness offered safety and the girls and their imperceptible guardian moved into the yawning portal, under the toothy rocks.

The two sisters silently moved through, working their way deep into the catacombs by running their hands along the wall, guiding them through the cavernous chambers. The eldest sister stopped suddenly and her sister thought that she heard their pursuers entering behind them, but it was deathly quiet. No. Her sister had seen something ahead. Something was guiding her, and in turn, her sibling, safely in.

The black statue began to grow heavy in the eldest sister's hands and she exchanged it to the other as it grew colder too. The feelings of nausea had returned, stronger than ever, and she stumbled as her limbs grew weaker. The obvious effect that the statuette was having was lost on the young girl, but not on Gam who scrutinized the scene in front of him, wondering why the father had seemed so unaffected by the statuette.

Suddenly the tell-tale sound of moving scree at the entranceway to the cave announced their pursuer's arrival. But the grey-skins never came.

There was loud grunting and the sound of a struggle - some sort of argument was taking place, an argument between two men. Over the prize inside perhaps? Gam wondered.

The rocky scree still fell under the struggling pursuer's feet and miraculously, or perhaps supernaturally, it loosened the small rocks at the opening and finally, they plummeted. The scree gave way to small rocks and the rocks to boulders.

When the dust cleared there was no sound coming from the arguing grey-skins, there was no moon illumination. There was nothing. The entrance was sealed tight.

They were safe. But they would die.

Soon, with her younger sister sleeping soundlessly, she let her head fall forward and with her forehead against the rock, she slept.

The statuette began to shed a mist that was both soothing and reassuring yet also threatening and angry, it encircled the girl, it offered her a safety of sorts and she murmured gently in her sleep. And then she screamed.

For a reason Gam could not comprehend she did not wake and as her screams grew distressing and chilling, her skin began to blister and peel and Gam back-peddled away - nearly falling - from the loathsome revelation, he suddenly awoke in his cot at the inn, fingers clutching a sodden blanket.

CHAPTER FOUR

29th Morn, Lunar Cycle of the Cursed Constellation,
1189 Winters.

The following morning after a cheerful breakfast which consisted of delicately-sweetened rye bread smothered with local honey and strawberries - which Bardon referred to as Pixie Bread - and washed down with copious amounts of Blueberry cider, Gam had set his mind to re-exploring the barrow.

The meal had been a great way to start any new day and after a good night sleep, well, after his chilling nightmare anyway, he thought fresh eyes were just the ticket to look over the barrow again.

The clouds had cleared and the glorious morning sun illuminated the high-set windows of the Fool's Nook and feeling rather chipper himself, considering all, he had been surprised to find Loewen still in her cot when the girl had not turned out for morning call. She looked quite pale and her features appeared moderately drawn. When Gam had felt her forehead it was very cold and clammy. Insisting she should stay in her cot, after Gam opened her window to allow fresh air in and maintain that she should sip warmed water, he left her to sleep.

He trod the rain soaked path out of Frostcross, reflecting on the girl and her ailment. He had been glad that Bardon had offered to bring her more hot water, just as he had reportedly done the night before and that settled the Friar's night time reservations.

After a reasonably pleasant jaunt, at least after venting some painful - and rather stinky - gut gas, he came to the mighty Oakstone and the barrow beyond. He decided that he should search the chamber that Loewen had originally yester noon, in case the apprentice had missed something unintentionally – he needed to be sure that she had done a thorough job and then he could put that nagging question out of his mind. Perhaps it was fortuitous that she had not accompanied him this day and he wouldn't have to risk hurting her feelings.

He lit his small lantern and pressed himself in through the low, moss-caped barrow entrance and emerged inside the entry chamber. The floor was still damp but the first thing that the Friar noted was that their footprints in the dirt and loose stone were gone, which meant someone, or something, had been here since, covering their own tracks and in the same instance obliterating all the recent activity. Gam frowned from this latest discovery and pressed in further, staying focused and aware in case the *something* still dwelt inside.

He crept cautiously through the gloom of the narrow passage grave, his lantern barely lit the recess of the rough hewn walls. The air was stale and still and the candle's flame was small because of it. He searched his hands over the walls, feeling for any type of obvious nook or cranny.

He shortly entered the burial chamber complete with its bloody residue – had the corpse been Jonah? If so, why was it missing? More questions flittered about his muddled brain. Gam rubbed his temples soothingly.

This chamber led to the polygonal chambers, where the hollows were broken up into segments by the low cross stone slabs. Gam took the smaller tomb, which originally Loewen had searched alone. He pressed himself into the first section, shining the lantern in all corners. He felt along the stone, looking for any hidden compartment, sweeping spider webs out of the way and remembering Loewen's yelp of surprise at finding one of the black-orbed and leggy denizens of the web.

He searched the last section, suspecting that this had been a stupid idea and all for naught, when he gently pushed the stone back. Pushed the stone back? That shouldn't be able to happen! He stopped and attempted it again and sure enough the rock moved back a little further. Soon something clicked and revealed a cube-like compartment within the stone, of approximately the size of a, of a, 'mead jug! There I go again, thinking of booze,' he chided himself.

"Hogsdung!" exclaimed Gam, "how on earth did the child miss this? I suppose that damned spider got her all jumpy from stickin' her little pinkies in the sections to search proper!"

Gam held up his lantern and shone it on the compartment as best he could. His heart sank – it was empty. "O blow it!" he cursed, smacking the side of the wall in annoyance. Another click followed, Gam stopped, eyes darting curiously, "what was that?" he breathed. The snap seemed to come from inside the compartment, or was it the wall adjacent to it? He slapped the stone wall again, nothing happened. Something inside told him to slap the rear wall of the compartment – that was where the noise had come from after all. He reached in and thumped the wall. The click reverberated all around him this time and there was an explosion of dust almost directly on top of him followed by a severe grinding noise. He yelped in fright as he nearly fell and disappeared through the wall which he was leaning against. He quickly regained his feet, to discover the opening of a secret passage. Blowing and waving the dust from his face, he lifted aloft the lantern - wondering what he might find - whilst his other hand went instinctively for his hammer shaft. He waited patiently whilst the dust cleared but nothing else happened, nor did anything assail him.

Cold, stale air sighed out of the opening. He quickly backed away to avoid breathing in the barrow air. Old, foul air could harm the unwary, so he decided to let the passage breathe while he sat a short distance away and ate a cold lunch. He stretched and thought he glimpsed a shadow slinking in the corner recess where there shouldn't have been one, but when he stared at the spot it was gone. Quickly chewing the last of his bun and swallowing it with a helpful and generous glug of mead, he gathered up his pack and quickly headed for the new passage.

He slowly shone the lantern in and around, and holding his breath, stepped though into the roughly-hewn passage and guardedly ventured on.

Gam arrived at what initially appeared as a junction; he moved through the thickening dust to the end and peered around each corner. The passage to his left seemed wrong and it was man-made unlike the main natural tunnel he had just traversed. His limited knowledge in intricate chapel masonry revealed faults in the lintel above. Gam crouched down, throwing his excess robe-end over one shoulder and withdrew the prong that he used for eating his trail rations. He pushed it into an area of loose stone on the ground, nothing happened. He did so again, one pace forwards, until finally a section sunk under the prong's weight. He instinctively stepped back; as expected, the wall suddenly collapsed to the floor. If an unsuspecting person had turned and wandered up the passage, they would have most certainly been crushed to death.

"Too easy!" His lips twisted into a smile that mingled triumph with contempt and, rather the smugger for it, sandled feet took him further down the passage as it grew slightly larger.

Gam's hands shortly ached with the cold and he shivered. He squinted into the blackness that surrounded him. When his eyes grew accustomed to the gloom, even with the lantern light, he saw that he was standing in a grander passageway. Rocks, large and misshapen, supported a rocky ceiling. It was only after a moment that Gam suddenly observed the ledges to his left and right stretching off down the passageway… and on those ledges were coffins. There were at least twenty or thirty, maybe more; coffins made of stone, wood, some gold and silver. Many were cracked and broken, their bony denizens hanging out of them, all leering at him with the ceaseless grin of death. Gam gulped deeply and padded down the passage, looking dead ahead, if he didn't look at them, maybe they would just stay set and unanimated. Yes that was the key – not to look. He gulped again and hurried on down the tunnel.

Somewhere in the distance a faint illumination spurred his optimism of an exit. As he vigilantly walked the nightmarish route the sense of the foreboding - an icy chill that felt more to do with the supernatural, than the temperature - stayed with him. Perhaps it was the passages location, settled with its natural design, or perhaps it was something else? Either way Gam boldly continued.

It was with relief and at the same time disappointment that his hunch of some valuable treasure residing on a neat little plinth, ripe for the taking, was ill founded. There was nothing here; it just opened out into daylight.

The area was hilly, patches of trees and shrubbery littered the region, blocking much of the landscape from Gam's view. He would have to be wary here, making navigational decisions as he cleared each clump of trees. He was limited to the route that wound around the trees. The hills had rocky faces that made them almost impossible to climb. He started out, staying silent. Low pine trees blocked a small valley, steep rocky hills rose on each side. The wind moaned over the bare stone and the ragged pinnacles. He was definitely heading downwards and the roar of the ocean was quite prevalent now, there seemed to be no way into this small mysterious valley other than the way he had come. Gam turned in a full circle scanning the countryside and carefully picked his way through the trees. Eventually he scrambled out from under the green canopies, plucking pine needles from his habit's hood.

A series of crystal clear, aqua blue pools - each seemingly more appealing than the last - were naturally formed in the grey rock, like oval bathtubs. The pools looked as if they must be warm so blue was their entrancing colour. They looked delightful, surrounded by a carpet of soft and springy green moss and ferns. One could imagine a mischievous sprite with the power to enthrall people, bewitching folk to take off their clothes and jump in.

A few trees stood sparse and leafless and Gam had the notion of hanging up his robe on a helpful branch and taking a plunge. Perhaps it *was* fairy mischief! He shuddered involuntarily and cast fleeting looks around him.

The crags sprouted long grass, thin heather and a few bramble bushes, set further away, but that was still not enough to save them from nimble fingers and Gam was unable to resist helping himself to several, dozen, or so, juicy blackberries.

Behind the brambles a rocky ledge met him, the waves of the sea gently lapped over the rocks and a further barrier of rock just beyond, protected the natural ledge. Still chomping blackberries, the first thing that occurred to Gam was how perfect the area was for a natural and protected launch for a small sailing vessel for smugglers, when, as he rounded the corner he came into sight of a small schooner. The ketch's sails were down and it was carefully tied up, gently bobbing in the natural cove. Gam went to ground and carefully looked over the area, but he was sure he was alone. This ship must be moored here for emergencies - though the trail was not well travelled at all. In all probability few, if any one else other than Jonah knew of this location at all. Therefore, presumably, Gam surmised, this schooner must belong to Jonah. Perhaps an urgent escape route, should he need it, moored in a still and secret cove, away from the rough Howl of the Ocean point.

Gam, now certain there was no one present, made his way to the light craft and explored the deck with his eyes, deciding not to venture on board. With his luck so far which consisted of finding the only root to trip over and the only splinter in a floor board to prick him - he was bound to end up in the salty brime. No, he had unearthed enough for now and until he could mull things over a little more he would keep this little fortuitous discovery to himself.

A jet-black rat appeared in between a cluster of fallen stones and skulked around Scarpel Rock. It's nose twitched as it ran between the collapsed stones, presumably sensing for danger. It stood on its hind legs as it detected the newcomer emerging from the barrow. The rat stretched up, smelling the air, it had found what it was looking for…

Gam stepped out from the barrow into the morning sunlight, glad to breathe the fresh air once again just as something hissed menacingly and made him stop dead in his tracks. He slowly glanced down and locked onto red, evil, eyes watching him. A large black rat, whiskers twitching in anticipation, tail dancing expectantly stood quite still on a grass over-grown stone to his right. Gam didn't move and regarded the vermin curiously; it was exactly like that which young Bethe had described in her diary.

He didn't dare move, the slightest twitch could trigger the rat into attack and he knew only too well the true nature of the fell creature regarding him. Things must have been desperate to see it out during the daylight. It hissed again baring it's yellow, sharp teeth.

'Too late', thought Gam, it was going to spring. Gam fell back releasing his hammer just as the rat sailed through the air – just missing him. It landed on the lintel stone above the barrow's entranceway and for some reason, turned and fled down the back of the barrow. Gam stood and regarded after it curiously.

'Why did it do that? Unless,' Gam thought, 'unless, I actually surprised the little brute and it's tryin' to flee to report my little unearthing.' The thought of this filled him with more dread than discovering the rat in the first place. He needed an advantage in this investigation and he felt with this discovery he may just have one, unless this rat-thing reported his sighting to it's wretched kin.

Swearing, Gam took off after the rat as it fled down the small pebbles that made up the rear of the barrow. He doubted whether he would be able to catch such a creature as he near bobbed and bounced over the ground, when he noticed a spot of blood on a rock which it had vaulted over – it was injured. He must have caught it with his hammer at their initial exchange at the entrance and he quickened his ungainly bound, eyes darting, hammer swinging.

The rat screeched as it dashed this way and that trying to throw off it's pursuer, but one of its legs was twisted and it was limping heavily now. It cleared a large rock, where it thought it might have lost its pursuer and took shelter at the foot of this large monolith, concentrating to change its form. It was only half transformed when repeated hammer strikes pounded it into a sickening tangled mass of scrawny human limbs and bristly rat flesh. Gam stepped back satisfied, looking at the remains with just one eye. Perhaps he had gone a little hysterical but the very notion of lycanthropy had always given him the willies and he was determined to flatten it with conviction. Still, the advantage was still with him - if he could only understand what all these discoveries meant and what tied them all together, he was sure he would get to the bottom of things. It was like owning all the pieces of a jigsaw puzzle but without knowing the picture and where to place them. A certain face popped into his mind - he knew it all just hinged on catching up with this perplexing Rake character.

"Ho there Gam," came a familiar voice as Gam cleared the Barrow fens, trudging ever on. "How goes the investigation?"

Gam looked up to regard the friendly face of Thesden. The warrior, turned farmer, pulled a small hand cart loaded with produce. Gam smiled with relief and bumbly shambled to meet him.

Thesden was on a very faint track above the old trail which wound higher up the hillside. Gam supposed that the view over the heathlands would have been spectacular on a clear day. "Slowly, I'm afraid."

"Did you catch up with Grim?" Thesden asked as Gam drew up next to him and took one of the cart handles. Thesden nodded his thanks.

"Nope, not yet - a lot has happened mind you and each discovery a little more perplexing than the last - I just need to tie them all together somehow," Gam enthused. "To be honest, I'm far keener to catch up with this Rake character!"

"Aye, Bardon mentioned him too. Tith said she saw the fella flittin' around town," said Thesden, adjusting his grip upon the cart.

"Really? When was this?" asked Gam. Thesden thought for a moment and then replied, "actually it must have been early eve - the day before you arrived."

Gam nodded, "I have other witnesses reporting t' have seen him then, including Bardon, who was near-threatened by the dastardly fellow."

"Really?" said Thesden, surprised. "The old goat never mentioned that!" He laughed out loud, "Well, I suppose he wouldn't admit to that, proud as he is, would he."

Gam smiled broadly.

"From how Tith described the fellow; tall, young, long dark hair, speaks better than I and thee-"

"Aye, that's him alright." Interrupted Gam, wondering where this was going and clearly recalling the description from his encounter outside the chapel.

"-Well, I'm not one to give miss-information, but he sounds awfully like a fella that lives at Cullakin."

Gam stopped, "Cullakin?"

"Aye, it's a small cottage up the coast from me, before one reaches Oscaig. I can't be sure, and I certainly don't wanna waste your time - or be seen to spread tales and all - but Cullakin has been empty for nay on two winters and then, all of a sudden, folk saw smoke comin' from the chimney, and a figure has been seen around the place - but up to now no one has addressed themselves in town as the new occupant. Kept to themselves see, but it's mighty curious that it coincides with the occasion that this Rake fella has been seen around Frostcross."

"That is indeed helpful information Thesden, and I thank ye for it. If it turns out to be for naught, I shan't say that it was ye good self that gave me the lead."

Thesden smiled and nodded, "I'm grateful." He paused in thought, "look, once I've delivered this cart to Frost' I would gladly lead you to the cottage if you like. Its not far outta my way home to Lon-Ban."

"I would be much obliged," replied Gam, as he guided the cart around a pot-hole.

"If you continue on the main coastal path," said Thesden pointing the way he had come. "You will eventually pass a small wood, a monument and then pass by an estuary, but keep on the track and eventually you will see a small sign and my humble farmstead of Lon-Ban. Continue on the track rather than taking the fork, until you come to a steep hill where there is an old ruined shack. I'll meet you there first light of morn and take you on to Cullakin. I'll be coming cross-country from Frostcross."

Gam's eyes widened with the prospect of another hike. "Not far then," he whimpered, "right, well, when ye get there, I'll be the one throwing up."

Thesden smiled as Gam offered a cheeky but jovial nod of half understanding, half thanks. He left the farmer to continue his delivery into town. Gam wondered if he should have asked Thesden to pass on a message to Loewen at the Fool's Nook, but decided that she should probably do well to spend the time recovering in her cot. He could spend the night at the chapel and be better set to depart well before first light in order to meet Thesden.

With a little more gusto to his step, he started along the cart track. The winding trail took him back to his adventuring days and the tunes he used to intone while treading the ends of the land in search of glory.

To the hills, toward the dales,
the mountains, sea, an' woodland ways,
follow the clouds, all the day, every night, till far away.
O steady is the mountain path, thou shalt seek the way,
burden and toil bears on the mind, thou shalt seek the way,
firm is thy tread, on trails of olde, thou shalt seek the way,
steady is the mountain path, thou finds a way.

***

The three Tralleign children and Dulwin, their new guide, followed the winding coastal trail. The track wound inland through the Barrowdale countryside as twilight shaded the sky. The wood began to grow sparse and the long downlands leading up to the peaks of Montasp came into view on the horizon.

Further along the trail they came upon a small shrine, standing alone by the side of the stony track, maybe thirty hands from the trail itself. Built of common stone from the area, it appeared to the children very old indeed. Cordale pointed it out to Dulwin, who was dressed in travelling clothes, with bedrolls, blankets and a bow strapped across his back. He utilised a long spear as a walking stick and a dagger rested in the top of his high boots.

The young boy ran across the grass to the shrine, momentarily faltering in a patch of muddy ground. He rubbed his hand over the strong weather-worn stone, inadvertently trampling the native plants beginning to creep over it.

"Come 'ere, young Cordale," called out Dulwin, half grinning, "that shrine is for the fallen Dalesmen that defended Hauntmouth against a fierce pirate raid. We lost near twenty lives that day."

Ysara looked vaguely shocked at the terrific loss of life - being the more sensitive of the children - and shot her brother a withering look, who in response returned from the shrine.

The respectful silence was broken as Bethe burst out laughing as Cordale, who slipped again in the mud, landed on his backside with a splash. Dulwin tutted, scratching his long beard and then went to assist the boy, half dragging him up by his cuff.

"I can manage!" protested the boy, loudly.

"Listen 'ere master Cordale, these lands can be very dangerous, especially to children. Let's not draw attention to ourselves, hey?"

Ysara shot her brother another warning look and the boy nodded in agreement. Bethe quietened too.

This water-logged ground was the edge of a small marsh and the trail actually formed the perimeter of a small estuary that ran all the way to the sea. This part of Barrowdale was very quiet except for the occasional bird call from the estuary. The four travellers felt very exposed and continued with little talking.

Dulwin seemed very distracted and concerned with their surroundings, perhaps even wary of something that could be following them. Bethe felt he was acting as adults do when something bothered them, yet did not want to alert the children for fear of scaring them. Recognising this behaviour however, caused her to be more alarmed but she shook the feeling aside and set her mind to distraction by counting the local avian life. Bethe's eyes followed the flight of some long-legged bird as it flew over the marsh to land on a wooden stump sticking out of the shallow bog adjacent to a small house coming into view positioned on short stilts.

The watery grassland stretched some two hundred yards away from the raised, rock-strewn trail. Tall grasses protruded above the water's surface, as did bushes and a few small trees. The house sat alone and dejected perhaps thirty yards away, its shutters down and door closed. The water nearby was disturbed as some small animal ducked under the surface as the travellers ventured by. A few regularly used campsites lined the trail-side but there was no path or dock, to suggest that the house was in use.

The guide hurried the children on without question, the eeriness of the place had chilled them all through and they quickened their pace to be away from this area before nightfall.

Dulwin explained that he was hoping to be a lot nearer to Frostcross before they bedded down and made camp - though that was looking a little optimistic - however, he pushed the children on a few hours longer than perhaps he would have normally done.

When they reached Frostcross, Rake had instructed Dulwin to hire a horse and wagon team to take the children to Cheth Chandor and await their father.

Soon they headed off the pebbly trail and made camp for the night under a large old tree. The moon was out - high and bright - and the children, laying out on their bedrolls, had fun in pointing out several bright stars, including the Dragon Heart Constellation.

Before they bedded down under the canvas tent that their guide had erected, the children emptied their pockets and softened up their packs to utilise as pillows. Cordale fell onto his bedroll and laid his weary head on the pack, only to rise quickly in annoyance as something hard dug into the side of his face. He shoved his hand into the pack and withdrew a small oblong parcel wrapped in a handkerchief. He grimaced on realising what the item was and discarded the package to one side in frustration. He laid his sleepy head back down on the now softer pack.

Ysara reached into her long traveling cloak and from it's deep pocket withdrew little Balthy and gave the little animal a small handful of nuts she had collected under the tree. She rested her head back and watched the golden animal tuck into its natural meal sitting upon her chest. Shortly, she and her brother and sister fell asleep, leaving their guardian keeping a furtive watch.

None of them noticed the handkerchief-wrapped parcel begin to glow and burn a small hole in the material, revealing it as Master Savant Ritic Vilan's Sorceries of The Wraith Tome, recovered from Cordale's Academy. Something was happening to it. Something, disturbing. The silhouette of a ghostly face began to appear on the cover - the Wraith's book of profane sorceries and demonology lore could sense the presence of undead.

***

That night something else nearby sensed the closeness of undead. The door to the strange little house on stilts, located in the middle of the marsh, opened menacingly and two pinpoints of burning red glared out from within.

After several moments a figure emerged onto the porch, human sized but still hard to discern in no more than the uncanny light given off by the emanating natural gases of the marsh. One thing was sure, the pinpoints of red were eyes and they surveyed the horizon with enormous interest, before a sneer gave way to revealing white, extended canine teeth.

With a flash off some notable edged weapon in its hands, the figure, cloaked in shadows, leapt from the doorway into the marsh and vanished - no splash followed - and even the nesting morass-avian in the nearby bush never knew anything had passed by.

***

It wasn't a shrill scream, a harrowing cry or even a surprised howl, but something of a sickening hack that made young Cordale startle awake and sit bolt upright. He urgently turned his head, wondering what distressing noise had startled him. His sisters were next to him, fast asleep, however his breath caught in his throat when he realised that Ysara was actually awake, her eyes wide open with terror and - judging by her stillness - holding her breath.

Cordale swung around to see what Ysara was staring at and attract their guide's attention, when he suddenly observed the vile vista that had rooted his sister to the spot. Some kind of haggard figure was bent over Dulwin, who was still sitting up against the tree by the dying embers of the fire.

A sickening sound emanated from the figure, like that of... Cordale couldn't place it. The figure straddling the guide was hard to observe in the darkness, only the glow from the embers revealed the scene at all. Cordale could just about see the guide's flailing arms as he tried to defend himself but he was just too weak to succeed. Dulwin must have been completely taken by surprise as he was still seated and his sword still sheathed. His body suddenly convulsed and a spasm spiralled jarringly down his arms. A whimper followed and then Cordale recognised the disgusting sound that had awoken him and it was comparable to the sound of pigs ravenously feeding on their first swill of the day. It was butchery.

Cordale abruptly spurred into motion and shoved the blanket away whilst paddling his legs to get him up quicker. Bethe had awoken and was acting with the urgency of her brother, however Ysara was still struck with paralysing fear, unable to take her eyes off the gruesome scene.

Dulwin was managing to murmur something. The futility of his defence, and obviously in suffering so much pain, he was unable to coherently speak with any articulation - but he was trying to say something.

Cordale and Bethe both grabbed at Ysara but the girl wouldn't move and then she yelped as something in her pocket bit her and made her start. Bethe took Ysara's head in her hands and forced her to look away from the gruesome display and into her eyes instead. Ysara complied and an instant later the three children were up, looking to each other for support and direction. Cordale grabbed at Dulwin's spear that was resting next to the tent and his sisters turned in behind him.

The suckling sound quietened as Dulwin continued to flay his arms and whimpered a string of sounds together as he urgently tried to talk.

Cordale began to advance slowly on the figure, the girls behind him. He could see that the figure was wearing an assortment of ragged clothing and its limbs were horribly disfigured - nevertheless presumably still functioning - yet how, Cordale could not say. The things eyes were wide and staring as if it had no eyelids. It was then that the boy realised the flesh of Dulwin's attacker was white, blotchy and blood stained in places. Cordale faltered and stopped as the attacker's head slowly began to turn toward them, revealing it's twisted, decaying features, sunken lidless eyes and inhumanly sharp, stiletto like teeth. The boy flinched as he could now clearly see Dulwin's half eaten face. Cordale cried out in shock, comprehending the scene. He noticed the guide's eyes open wide when he too, in turn, could now see the children from behind his attacker and he desperately managed to cry what he had been trying to communicate previously.

"RUN!" he shouted as he clamped his arms around the undead creature, determined to give the children time to escape whilst his ebbing strength allowed it.

Acting on fear and impulse, Cordale dropped the spear, grabbed his sisters and yanked them away. The undead creature struggled in the dying Dulwin's grip, it shrieked into the night sky, crying out in annoyance.

The children sped off into the night as the undead creature turned once again on Dulwin, biting and hacking as it urgently tried to free itself from the dying man's grip. As much as Dulwin tried, under the brutal punishment he was taking, he soon expired and his grip went limp. Shrieking with the pleasure of success, the creature pulled a dagger out from between it's ribs where Dulwin had managed to stab it during the struggle. The undead abomination howled as it lurched with disturbing speed and gave chase after the three Tralleign children.

***

Ysara, once away from the horrific creature and their brutally murdered guide, soon became a little calmer and guided Bethe and Cordale behind a cluster of thick gorse bushes. She and Bethe were breathing fast, tears streaming their faces, but Cordale was surprisingly quiet. Though Bethe decided that it was with shock.

"W..What was that?" Bethe dared to whisper. Ysara shook her head negatively and they both traded glances and then fixed young, scared eyes on their brother.

"I don't know!" he exclaimed, scanning the darkness for the creature, "it was like a walking, disfigured corpse!"

Cordale's entire complexion had changed from a healthy pink to a deathly pale shade of grey. He then transfixed Bethe with an intense stare, "I think it was what father calls the undead."

Ysara frowned at her brother's words but before she could comment, Bethe pushed them both into a run, "t..the creature's c..coming!"

Running breathlessly down a particularly narrow path into a deep wood the children came upon a clearing some thirty-five feet wide. A huge oak tree stood alone at the centre of the clearing, its branches spanning more than the thirty-five feet to either side of its massive trunk. The gnarled trunk itself was huge, and its roots broke the surface reaching across the clearing. The tree stood as a king over its neighbours and the other trees had grown around the edge of the clearing, as if leaving a respectful distance to the oak tree. A disease seemed to have ravaged the centre of the tree, leaving a not so obvious hollow in its centre but this was lost to the children as they near tumbled into the centre of the clearing to escape the pursuing creature.

The undead abomination was close; as soon as it caught sight of the children - rather than just smelling their wake - it began it's spine-tingling howl.

The children scrambled away but it looked like they would only get halfway across the clearing before the creature would catch them. Bethe began whimpering, comprehending their certain horrific demise at the hands of this nightmarish thing and she began to sob for her father. Her own tears blinded her and she tripped on one of the oak roots. In the desperate urgency to balance herself, she tripped again and landed hard, sprawling in a heap amongst the roots. Ysara wiped the sweat from her face, turned and screamed for her to rise. She could see the approaching creature and screamed with further urgency, encouraging her sister to stand and continue running. Realising that Bethe was injured, Ysara ran back to assist her, shouting for Cordale to help but the boy seemed rooted to the ground with fear. Ysara reached Bethe and started to pull her screaming sister up, shouting at her to rise. Bethe shrieked again as the creature closed, moving with steady, if ungainly, speed over the tree roots. Ysara's encouraging shouts turned into screaming orders. They staggered back together as the creature reached out to ensnare them, so close that they could smell the fetid stink of its breath coming from a red-stained, slobbering mouth that encased partly broken, vicious teeth. Bethe was kicking her feet at the creature, Ysara was hauling her backward and screaming for their brother, the end was close, there was surely no way to escape now. Ysara started screaming uncontrollably as the abomination swiped at Bethe's kicking foot and caught it. The undead creature howled in pleasure and stretched its other long-nailed hand toward Ysara, as Balthy swiftly appeared from her pocket and bit the creature, causing it to recall and violently shake it's hand. The poor little animal went flying across the clearing to land somewhere amongst the roots and Ysara cried out again. But Balthy had bought them a precious few moments.

The Sovereign Oak Glade was echoing with the sound of screams, from both the mortal and the undead.

As the girl's screams reached a crescendo and the creature lunged at them with saliva dripping in ravenous anticipation, a deep hoarse call from somewhere to their left silenced the children's screams.

A large figure rushed into the clearing and both Ysara and Bethe held their breath, and each other, their desperation for a saviour did not allow them to comprehend another possible foe and they launched themselves away from the undead creature as it barely had time to turn in response to the raining silver death from above. The figure brought its weapon - a hammer Ysara observed, crashing down into the undead being. The foul creature, so taken with its next meal, had no time to raise to meet the blow and it took it full force against it's shoulder. The gruesome crack of bone echoed around the clearing followed by a guttural howl.

Bethe screamed at the horrific sight and at last managed to stand and stagger back with her sister.

"Fear not children; move back whilst I finish this walking monstrosity!" came their saviour's words.

The man wasn't tall, he wasn't particularly young or old, but he was plump and very angry and the children observed him wield his huge hammer with natural grace, as if the weapon were a mere extension to his arm. As they watched, his angry expression turned to a smile and he beheld the children with friendly eyes even under the pressure of the combat.

"Stinks a bit, don't it!" he exclaimed, trying to waft the air in front of his nose. He smashed the creature again causing it to stagger back and in turn deftly avoided a sharp, taloned-hand swiping for his head. The children, still staring in shock, observed the portly fellow take a swig from a wine skin, stamp on the creature's leg - pinning it to the ground - and smash his hammer repeatedly against it's head, each time caving it in a little further.

"With the power of mead, I shall succeed!" Gam announced bludgeoning the ghoul's head in, "try and eat little children now will ye?"

Gam was initially surprised to find a lone ghoul attacking three children in the middle of a wooded clearing far from any habitated region. But then, so far on this trip, he had been surprised many times before and he was sure this wouldn't be the last. And he was right, for as he desisted his attack, certain that the ghoul was pummelled beyond recovery, a startled scream from one of the girls corrected his judgment.

The animated corpse had been lifeless for sometime and as he expected not much blood gushed from the deformed stump that was all that was left of its head but yet the creature was still moving. It rose and staggered around the uneven ground wildly, swiping its arms in an attempt to combat the friar.

The two girls embraced each other and the oldest turned her sister's head away, but went on to watch with morbid fascination.

Gam looked on, slightly befuddled and shouldered his ornate hammer. He placed his hand deep inside his worn satchel, muttering as to where the blessed water dwelt. He exclaimed in success and withdrew a clay and corked vessel and tossed it directly at the ghoul's chest where it shattered. In response the creature howled in pain and careered around, kicking out. In the space of a heartbeat, the ghoul's chest split wide open as sure as if done by some unseen axe, sending nauseating gases into the air.

Ysara gagged, holding Bethe tightly and screamed as the creature's ribcage broke wide open and then fell away leaving a gaping hole in its chest. Gam exploited the weakness and buried his hammer forcefully into the ghoul's very core. With that the undead creature finally expired, the necromantic enchantment contained within, destroyed.

"Rest, Jonah," Gam whispered. "Strong dark enchantments raised this poor wretch." he uttered to himself more than the children. His first thoughts were to how this old murdered sailor had come to be here, in this walking-dead state. This puzzle was growing far more complex than he originally thought.

Ysara and Bethe, who were beginning to calm with the threat passed, slowly stepped back to stand with Cordale who was emerging from behind a large, rising root, still clutching the half-wrapped tainted book of sorceries.

The Sovereign Oak Glade was tranquil and quiescent once again.

Bethe was the first to step up and she simply uttered, "thank you," in a quiet but steady voice. Ysara nodded but then scrambled to the far side of the clearing looking for Balthy.

"Ho there young-uns, ye be welcome. I'm guessing that you are Bethe, that you are Cordale and you," began Gam, pointing to the young girl scurrying amongst the roots to reclaim an uninjured Balthy, "are Ysara?"

Bethe nodded in puzzlement as Cordale stepped up to stand alongside his sister.

"My name is Gam, and I believe these are yours," smiled the friar handing over a tatty fistful of diary pages. "Now come with me, we must leave this place before more foulness arrives and we have much to talk about."

***

Alone in the Sovereign Oak Glade another figure stood in silence, observing from the hollow of the oak tree itself. Pin points of crimson the only tell-tale of it's existence.

A suffocating presence emanated from the being, a chilling evil that unmercilessly stabbed out at any form of life adjacent to it, even the hanging foliage withered and died under it's breath.

It had witnessed everything, from the children's arrival, the attack of the ghoul to the subsequent arrival of the young-ones saviour. At last, something of interest after all these seasons haunting the Dale. The being's breath fogged the air as it let out a wicked chuckle and licked the tip of a canine tooth.

***

Thesden met Gam as he had promised at a shack where the coastal trail forked at a small sign announcing the area as Cullakin. Gam introduced him to the Tralleign children and as they walked the stony, grass-edged cart track -where large puddles of water collected - they told him their frightful tale. Thesden's eyes were wide throughout most of the tale.

Last night seemed like a lifetime ago now, riding as they were in glorious sunshine, only the occasional lone cloud marring the otherwise azure sky. The sea gently lapped at the pebble-strewn beach to their right beneath the small cliffs and the sun glinted on the wave crests like a row of twinkling diamonds.

This area of relatively flat and springy under-foot grassland served as a wide plato leading up to steeper hillocks on their left and served as a natural area for the small farmsteads that worked the land.

The grass became a lot shorter due to the blackhead sheep that constantly grazed over the immediate land. Areas of sporadic and dense long grass littered the region, intermixed with young ferns and cotton grass. Occasionally a strong breeze disturbed the somewhat furry flower and sent its seeds dancing across the narrow track. Gam was very suddenly aware of why people like Thesden toiled to build a life for themselves here. Someway up the coast resided the busy city port and province of Morth Mortu which was well known to be responsible for forced human displacement, local poverty, indigenous crop destruction and environmental Armageddon. No wonder the Dalesmen and Chandorians alike stayed distant and isolated from the rest of the country.

Gam snapped out of his reverie by Thesden raising his hand in acknowledgment to a distant figure silhouetted against the sky on a high hillock. Smoke began to waft freely, spiralling up to the clear sky from a small mound adjacent to the figure.

Thesden felt Gam's eyes on him, "that's Sinton; he farms the kelp from the coastline."

Thesden noticed a slight frown furrow the Friar's brow, "the seaweed that clings to the rocks!" Gam smiled and nodded his thanks.

"The seaweed is gathered, collected and burned down in large piles, Abyss-of-a-job, but it eventually burns down to kelp ash which he sells to Alchemists for a reasonable sum in the city but it takes a lot of weed for the smallest amount of ash."

"Do many folk farm the kelp?" asked Gam.

"Nah, he's the only one in these parts. There aren't that many farms in Barrowdale so we don't really overlap; in fact we sometimes help each other out depending on the season. There are about six small farmsteads and crofts running down Barrowdale's coast to Frostcross. Two of them focus on fishing off the point and Danick - up yonder at Oscaig - peat smokes some of their catch. He collects the peat from the Meddle, dries, stacks it and uses it to smoke the salmon and trout for market – the nobility love it. Oscaig is the furthest farm and Danick is quite an independent and wild sort of fellow, you can recognise him from his tall frame, long hair and wild beard. Others are cattle and sheep herders – you'll see plenty of sheep round these parts!"

Gam could just about make out smoke from the chimneys of the small cottages of Bracken, clustered close to one side of a valley amid tall trees of Silver Birch and Ash.

"Though, come to think of it," continued Thesden, "I'm not sure what Rake's profession is?" he sighed, slightly puzzled, "still, guess we'll find out soon enough."

They all carried on down the stony track and Gam chuckled as he observed a lamb scratching its ear against a small cairn of rocks that may have once been an outhouse or shed and then - surprised at their sudden appearance - took off after it's mother. The skittish lamb soon shot under it's mother harrying her with it's keenness to suckle milk. Gam realised the little one's success as it's tail darted into a joyous waggle. The children laughed, momentarily being able to forget their nightmarish encounter.

Soon Rake's white-washed cottage came into view, perched on the cliff top overlooking a small sandy bay. A small fence marked the garden boundary all the way around where variegated small trees and bushes grew like a sanctuary away from the wild heather, gorse and long grasses. As they approached, opening a large field gate at the end of the track and picketing their mounts, Gam could clearly see the little garden area and stared at the forget-me-nots bobbing their blue heads over the fence. It was extremely well kept and all the flora had its own particular space – it looked more like an orderly city garden belonging to some noble or merchant's villa and though beautiful it looked a little delicate and out of place amongst such a rugged setting. The surprise flashing across Thesden's eyes was not lost on the monk either.

The grazing sheep near the fence glanced up as they approached and then warily and wearily wandered out of the immediate vicinity, heads dropping down to the grass once again. As Gam reached for the latch on the small gate, a cheeky notion occurred to him, where he would let the sheep pass their nemesis gate in order to get to the lush grass and tasty buds beyond. He was reminded again that this immaculate cottage with its neat and protected grounds belonged to someone who did not necessarily live here by choice.

Telling the children to follow behind he and Thesden carefully pushed open the wooden cottage door - which was not locked - and entered.

They stepped through a small porch, which apart from a small stack of kindling was bare. A small pair of antlers graced one of the walls and daisy chain stretching from rafter to floor dangled on a peg but judging by the lack-luster colours, had been there for some time. Gam cautiously pushed open a second door which led into the entrance hall and the first thing that struck him was the smell of soot. Dark wood paneling surrounded them and a detailed and quite true to life painting of a family hung directly ahead. The picture was oddly haunting, three old women sat in front of a man of equal age, a younger couple and finally two children to one side –

three generations sat for the artist in front of this very cottage. As Gam stepped in he was sure one of the old women's eyes followed him, eyes boring holes into his very soul - either her spirit was angered at his and Thesden's trespassing or his own conscious was prickling. The wood paneling opened out toward their right and turned into a dark wood and polished staircase. Two lanterns hung from brackets on either side of the opening. To their left looked to be the food preparation area and what looked like a very large table. It was old and to Gam's mind possibly quite valuable – it looked almost out of place in the simple setting of the cottage. Heading for the staircase Gam glanced into the room to their immediate right. It was a simple sitting room consisting of several sturdy and worn leather-wrapped chairs facing a large fireplace, where flames no longer licked but the embers still looked quite hot. A colourful rug lay at the foot of one chair and deer skin at the foot of the other. Many small pictures graced the walls all around the fireplace – the focal point, and a stack of old tomes sat precariously between the snug chairs. This was clearly a room often inhabited. The companions eyes were dragged away from the idyllic setting of the room to the stairs again as a light commotion was coming from somewhere above.

Gam and Thesden cautiously scaled the well-worn staircase and as they reached the top, Gam saw a blur of movement from one of the two bedrooms from the top of the stairs. He carefully placed a foot on the top step and edged around the newel post in order to catch a glimpse into the room. Sneaking up on some poor sod in his home was not his preferred way of a greeting but in this instance and with all the suspicions cast upon the individual herein, it was necessary.

He looked in to the room to see a smallish trunk on the cot which was being hurriedly packed by a figure all too familiar to Gam. He was tall, with long hair, Gam was sure the ladies would find him a handsome sort and he was dressed in leather breeches and a raggedy shirt, that probably once would have been the height of city fashion. Gam could see a silver icon hanging from a thong around his neck as he leant over the trunk but then his most recognisable features became apparent as he suddenly looked straight at Gam at the top of the staircase. Bright green eyes – it was Rake.

A flash of alarm from those eyes sent Rake into a flurry of movement. The trunk lid was slammed shut, a saber lifted from the bed and he thrust through the doorway straight at a wide-eyed Gam who back-peddled, rushing to lift his hammer and stepping back onto Thesden coming up the stairs. The farmer called out and slipped, taking Gam down a step and therefore enabling Rake to squeeze by. However, at seeing Thesden, Rake faltered and slowed, "You! Why are you here? I've seen you in Frostcross – you're a crofter here, no?"

Before Thesden could compose himself from the slip and respond, Gam was on Rake and pinned him up against the wall with his tremendous bulk.

"Got ye, yer little bugger! I'm taking ye in for the murder of Jonah!" Gam announced, puffing a little.

"Murder? Of Jonah? No, n..no! You've got it all wrong!" replied a startled Rake. "Forgive me for saying, but I could take you in a heartbeat and be gone, but let me explain!"

Gam squinted, there was something about his bearing that made Gam think that perhaps this wasn't the best position to be in, he followed Rake's eyes down and saw that he had an ornate, long-bladed dagger thrust up against the Friar's ribs. Gam then felt the point.

"Well, pup, it seems I'm all ears," he said, loosening his hold. Thesden then saw the threatening dagger and held his glaive up menacingly.

"I am not the man you seek. But I can understand your reasons for thinking that I am. Like you, I was under the misapprehension that maybe *you* were not as you seemed. I may have been wrong and I am willing to parley and explain things to you," uttered Rake. He slowly moved the dagger away and held it and his other hand high, yielding his strong position. He offered the same to Thesden and in response the warrior, come farmer, lowered his glaive. Gam nodded, "go on."

"I am from a noble family of Cheth Chandor. For quite sometime now I have been wandering the land with little choice since a killer escaped from custody and swore revenge against me, me as the one who had originally caught him and presented him to the militia. I came here to Cullakin to settle down, as it is not known that my family own it. It used to belong to Dulwin..." Thesden nodded in agreement to Gam at this point. "...who worked for my father."

"So ye are in hiding?" said Gam very matter-of-factly. Rake nodded, "Aye, for a time and until the killer is caught again. His presence reaches far and I alone could not hope to defeat him again." Rake added, as if he needed to explain his craven concealment. "I was here for sometime before I thought it safe to visit Frostcross, I longed for company and I stupidly let my guard down and subsequently paid for it. There was an old seaman drinking there and our eyes met across the busy taproom. It was Jonah. I recognised him immediately and I witnessed a flash of recognition across the old pirate's lidless eyes."

"So some old buccaneer recognised ye, what does that matter?" asked Gam.

"Have you ever heard of a pirate captain known as the Wraith? And how he escaped from the gallows at Cheth Chandor and that he swore revenge against his captor?" Rake asked.

"Of course, against Raklen Mortlake, everyone knows that, even the wee young uns – told over story time- wait! You?" Gam exclaimed.

"Aye," replied Rake nodding slowly and glancing down. "For my troubles. I am Raklen Mortlake." He lifted the silver icon hanging on the thong that was inside his shirt. It clearly showed the Mortlake emblem of a Keep by a lake.

Thesden looked stunned and uttered, "I used to serve in the militia and thought I recognised the famous Mortlake chin!"

"Jonah was a member of the Wraith's crew and had been a pirate all is life. In fact he was the only survivor of a pirate raid against Frostcross many, many winters ago, even before the Wraith's time.

I was sure that he would report his discovery of me to his former captain, in order to re-gain his favour, ever since he failed his watch and the Wraith cut off his eyelids."

"So ye killed him?" asked Gam through clenched teeth. Raklen looked shocked.

"No, not at all! I decided that I should meet with him, maybe pay for his silence but when I found him he was already dead, I swear it. I panicked thinking the Wraith was already here."

Gam nodded, "where did the body go?"

Raklen shrugged his shoulders and sighed. "I know not, I looked for him. I even approached you at the chapel to see what you knew." Gam nodded, remembering.

"Either way, I do not believe the Wraith is here yet, fore I still live. I have been hunted by creatures so evil that they can surly only be minions of that devil of a man and I am sure it was one of those that dispatched Jonah. Though for exactly what reasons, I do not know."

"Why didn't ye confide in me Raklen?" asked Gam, giving the noble a little more space.

"For all I knew you were with the Wraith or working for him - you did arrive in Frostcross at the time of the murder. My father, Lord Mortlake told me to trust no one!"

Gam's eyes twinkled and he looked momentarily distracted but he quickly composed himself, listening to Raklen.

"I do not like this sudden insurgence of undead and other filth in Barrowdale. He is getting close to me, I can feel it. He got close to me once before, near the caves of the Dead Maw Lake, and it felt just like this. I must go, not for my sake but for the folk of the Dale. It will not just stop with my demise but the entire dale will suffer for it, just because I attracted him here. I am sure his assassin murdered Jonah - maybe some other old crew mate? All I can think is that he was murdered to stop him exposing this assassin working for the Wraith." Raklen finished.

"I wonder if it could be that dwarf, Grim?" speculated Gam. "He's old enough to have known Jonah back then and he's always watching everyone and everything - gives me the heebie-jeebies!"

"I'm not so sure," offered Thesden, leaning his glaive against the handrail and taking out a long pipe. "Jonah's habited Frostcross for many winters - surely something would have happened between him and Grim before, they often frequented the Fool's Nook together."

Gam pursed his lips but thought better of retorting for once. His lips then formed into a thin smile. "Well Raklen, there are some here that will be mighty pleased to see ye again and it would sure convince me if yer tale is true or not."

Raklen looked puzzled.

"Children," called Gam. "Would ye come in here?"

Bethe, Ysara and Cordale stepped into the entrance hall looking around wide-eyed. As soon as their eyes fell upon the Mortlake noble, beaming smiles flowered from their faces and they exclaimed his name together. Bethe ran forward and hugged him.

"Rake, it is you, it is. I am so happy to see you again. Did you get away from the ratmen? How is your wound?" asked Bethe suddenly remembering. As Cordale joined his sister at Raklen's side he Spotted Gam holding his hammer and Thesden, with his glaive in easy reach. The boy suddenly realised the Friar and Farmer's intent.

"No! You can't Gam - he saved us!" exclaimed Cordale stepping onto the staircase and squeezing between Gam and Raklen. The noble looked both surprised and touched. Bethe and Ysara then caught onto their brother's observation and crowded around Raklen as well. Thesden chuckled and Gam waved his hands fussily.

"Aye, its alright little Tralleigns - I read your diary too remember and I know what good he did!"

Gam squeezed back down the staircase to join Thesden, glad to be out of the close confinement.

Raklen smiled and ruffled Cordale's hair and gave Bethe and Ysara a hug, "it is good to see you all again. I am glad you are safe and well - have you managed to contact your father?" Then Raklen wavered and asked, "if you are here, where is Dulwin?"

The children grew quiet and a tear rolled down Bethe's cheek. "He's d..dead," she uttered quietly.

Gam studied Raklen, carefully reading his emotions. He observed both anger and regret. Silenced reigned - Raklen set his hand into a fist and looked away. It seemed like an age passed as no one knew what to say and they slowly filed back down the staircase to stand in the entranceway.

"Let us all get back to Frostcross," announced Gam. "Ye must come too, where we can keep an eye on you - for good or bad, besides, if ye are telling the truth, as I believe, ye will be safer with us in numbers Raklen."

"I don't disagree Gam but the Wraith will be closing in, of this I am sure and I tire of running. It is not the place for the children though." Intoned Raklen, placing his hand on Bethe's shoulder.

"Well they can't stay here either!" returned Gam, rubbing his second chin thoughtfully.

"I have a horse and cart," offered Raklen. "Let them go to Cheth Chandor now and find their father."

"On their own? No it's far too dangerous, how about my cottage at Lon-Ban it's well protected?" suggested Thesden. "Besides, it is on our way. We can take your cart Raklen, and the children can take it to Lon-Ban - they will be safe there until all this blows over. I have plenty of food, a good stock of fire wood..."

The three men looked to each other, to the children and then nodded in agreement. As they gathered their belongings for the hike to Frostcross via Lon-Ban in silence, perhaps preparing themselves for what lay ahead, none witnessed a curious little Balthy sneak from Ysara's pocket and jump into Gam's baggy hood.

As Cordale re-shouldered his pack, he suddenly exclaimed at its weight. It was an accidental statement but one that was to shake Raklen to his core.

"O Piffle! This bloody book is so 'eavy!" the boy called out and then quickly remembered his place. "Sorry, but it *is so*!" He took a large leather-bound tome from the pack, which up to now Gam had been wondering what laid therein.

Raklen's eyes lit up, "what is this, pray tell!" The noble couldn't help himself and snapped up the book from the boy's grasping hands.

"It is but a long story Rake, I mean Raklen," started Bethe. "It belonged to an old Master Savant of Cordale's, from his old schooling house outside Cheth-"

"Gods above!" exclaimed Raklen, cutting off the girl. "Do you know what this is – who it belonged to?"

Cordale shook his head, "I know it's bad is all!"

Raklen handed over the old occult manual to Gam, eyes wide. The Friar took the book, merely glancing over it. He flicked through the first few pages and his eyes snapped open, "I say!"

CHAPTER FIVE

30th Eve, Lunar Cycle of the Cursed Constellation, 1189 Winters.

Louie Dafoe stepped out of the Cherub 'n' Chutney tavern that half leant against a thick buttress on the northern stonewall of Cheth Chandor - near the gateway - ten silver crowns the lighter on liquors for him and his acquaintances. He paced away from the old tavern and sought the lane that meandered through the little houses and miner's sheds that littered the region. They clung to the trail and grew sparser the further he walked away from the city walls, till eventually only one or two of the miner's sheds were visible adjacent to the trail that wound onward and down through the mountains to Barrowdale. The mining sheds were a bustle of activity in the morning but now they were relatively lifeless.

He was expecting the infrequent stage from Barrowdale that was due to reach Cheth Chandor shortly. It always entered through the south gate and stopped at the Picket Post Tavern and Fest Hall for unloading supplies, changing horses and coach master, before setting off again.

Today, he had it on authority that a very special person was taking the supposedly safe stage to Cheth Chandor, someone that Louie was extremely looking forward to meeting in person, and as soon as he reached a cluster of trees at the trailside he took out his disguise.

Leaving the cover of a large tree that stooped over the trail like a hunched old man a ten-breath later, Louie was dressed in a large black cape - with silver woven initials - a kerchief to cover the lower part of his face, eye mask and black tricorn hat complete with marabou and silver trim. *He* was the infamous highwayman of the Barrowdale to Cheth Chandor trail, Louie Dafoe, one hundred gold crowns on his head - wanted dead or alive. He gave a dry chuckle as he ripped a wanted poster down from the gnarled tree trunk.

Louie was expecting the rich merchant wife Rena Jhessel, who had recently taken residence in a large manor and estate, nestled at the foot of the mountains. She would never leave home without looking her best, which meant expensive rings, earrings, toe rings...

"And quite the gorgeous lass too," Louie whispered. He fancied himself quite the charmer and he was very proud that not one of his rich lady victims had ever actually raised charges against him - it had been their husbands!

Lord Mortlake wanted him for murder but that was just made-up propaganda by an irritated and blustering wind-bag of a noble who had his nose put out in failing to catch Louie when his wife was robbed, 'so courageously', thought Louie. As always, he was very much looking forward to meeting this beautiful Lady in person.

He ducked behind the large old tree and waited for the stage's arrival, behind his disguise one could not see the broad, beaming smile. The smile of a man who revelled in his work.

The Highwayman held his breath as he heard the stage and horse team rumbling toward him. Yes, that was definitely it. He drew out his two loaded hand-crossbows from under his capacious cloak and trying to contain his winning, gentleman thief smile, stepped out from behind the tree.

Expecting to see the lone stage trundling toward him - carrying the beautiful and rich Lady Jhessel - instead however he was met with a scene of bewildering content. A dozen or so pirates, judging by their garb, were charging after the stage as it sped toward him. The stage driver was shouting for help toward the mining sheds and cracking his whip at the horse team. The stage was covered in protruding crossbow bolts - making it look like a pincushion on wheels. As it drew closer, Louie could see that one of the deadly missiles was lodged in the driver's shoulder and he was having a hard time keeping control of the swiftly moving stage as it bounced on the rough track. The violent shaking of the stage drew a lady's scream from inside, and then, another.

Louie stood in shock, staring at the scene and bellowed, "Lady Jhessel! I'm coming!" Who were these evil tyrants that dared scare and come between him and his comely target? Who could do such a thing to so lovely a lady? Then he smiled in irony and ran toward the stage, he doubted they had ever tangled with the likes of him, Louie Dafoe, gentleman thief.

It was then that he noticed the large body of men moving down from the mountain's rivulets like rats. There must have been at least sixty or so, all looked to be coming from the direction of the Dead Maw lake and cave system – the only place large enough to hide such a large body of men Louie realised. As he stared harder, he noticed a man on a beast of a black horse who wore a metal mask in the shape of a leering ghost.

"T..The Wraith!" he stuttered and involuntarily shuddered, as he watched the main contingent of pirates, threatening and sinister, jog into the ditches to each side of the trail heading for Barrowdale. Whatever their intentions he found himself thankful that he did not reside in Barrowdale.

Instantly deciding that his own skin was far more important, he blew a kiss toward the open window of the stage as it shot passed and he thought he saw the most beautiful face in the world smiling and blowing a kiss back. But then, Louie was the kind of person who when engaged in taproom talk had seen and witnessed everything there was to see.

"Beautiful Lady Jhessel," he moaned in despair. "All those rings and things..." Not looking back and glad to have not tangled with the murderous cutthroats behind, Louie Dafoe, the innocent wooer of the female sex, set off at a sprint back to Cheth Chandor like a whipped cur.

***

Faint light showed from a few shuttered windows and a lantern swung in the wind as Gam approached the stone-flagged causeway of Rotten Row at the edge of Frostcross. A low moan brought Gam's attention to the corner of one of the first stone outbuildings. Before Gam had time to warn Thesden and Raklen - who were scouting the immediate area for signs of the Wraith or his pirates - he discerned movement dead ahead.

With rheumy eyes blazing with the malevolence that all undead regarded the living, two creatures staggered into the clearing. One of the creature's stomachs had split and its internal organs spilt out through the tear, glistening with sickly fluids. Their flesh was hanging limply off their rotting bones.

"Zombies!" Gam exclaimed, waving his hand in front of his nose at the stink. Something about the first zombie looked almost recognisable and he realised it was the farmer who had died in the wagon accident - why was he not buried, who or what had raised this poor wretch?

Gam ducked the zombie farmer's wild swing, grasped his old hammer and struck. The hammer impacted with it's head and span it away with a sickening wet thud. Steadying from the blow, Gam paced after the zombie, not wishing to give it time to retaliate and swung again.

Fighting tactics had taught him to exploit his enemy's weakness and their lack of speed had given him valuable insight.

The zombie recovered quicker than he might have expected however and the hammer only caught it a glancing blow. The zombie's head shuddered from the impact and it faltered and fell, spasms racking it's disgusting and rotting body.

Gam turned and side-stepped the other zombie's swinging arm, as it looked to rake him with pox-ridden, long fingernails. In too close after defending against the first zombie, Gam shouldered it to the side and released his elbow into its face with terrific force and then followed up, launching his hammer violently into it's face. The zombie fell away, clawing at the ground with a broken neck and smashed face; it would not stand in a hurry from the horrific wound. Gam stepped up to the first floored zombie and stamped down hard on its neck to incapacitate it too.

Sighing and blessing the two poor wretches as what was left of the corpse's continued to twitch on the ground, he unstoppered a small oil-container, retrieved from his pack and in turn earlier, from Gutso's store. Ceremoniously spilling the black liquid over the two zombies he sparked a flame and dropped it onto them.

"May they burn and at last rest in peace from the cleansing flames."

As Gam approached the Fool's Nook Inn he noticed it was darker than normal and eerily quiet. He approached cautiously and hesitated for a brief moment as he spied a figure leaning against the stone reveal of the doorway to the inn. As he drew closer the figure chuckled, a light feminine snigger.

"Loewen? Is that ye girl?" he asked, squinting into the darkness as she was leaning back nonchalantly and therefore in the shadow of the stone reveal. If it was her she didn't respond but another, somewhat sinister chuckle followed.

As Gam stepped up, he could make out petite, slender and exquisite features. Her eyes were mysterious, her luminous skin a pale hue, lips pouting, her well-defined face even more noticeable with her cropped pixie-like haircut. A black rat sat upon her shoulder, it's tail twitched as it regarded him, staring with beady, red eyes. She no longer wore the Tinhallow acolytes robe but instead a simple black garment, that perhaps revealed a little too much chest, waist and lower back than was acceptable. It was Loewen alright but there was something very wrong with how she looked. The girl was pale in the lamp light, her features were drawn and she had dark circles under her eyes. However, it was the look in those staring owl-like eyes that spooked Gam and her stance betrayed a confidence of that which he had never overly witnessed from her before - she appeared settled and comfortable with herself. Gam was just about to speak when he was joined by Raklen and Thesden, and then Loewen spoke.

"Well done, you fat fool," she said evenly to a very startled Gam. "You found him and brought him here. That will save me any further effort – my father will be pleased."

"What is this!" exclaimed Raklen to Gam. The Friar went to utter something but then stopped, suddenly all the pieces fell into place in a sudden whirlwind of realisation.

Loewen took delight in the Friar's expression of comprehension and intoned;

"Incy wincy necromancer stalks into the den,
out rush the Dalesmen to crush the undead men,
but with the stupid Dalesmen does the plan fall foul,
now further into their lair does the Wraith's daughter prowl.

My Ratmen and new undead thralls would have found dear Mortlake sooner or later, but thanks to you, here he is before me! I must congratulate you on behalf of my father. And he will be o so pleased to think that I have found you out!"

Raklen looked to Gam, "I take it this is all a surprise to you Gam?" he asked, lowering his hand to his sword and glancing around nervously. When Gam didn't reply he looked to his face and saw the Friar's perplexed expression. That at least spoke volumes.

"Just how in all things abyss-like did this happen?" asked Thesden, not privy to Gam's bewildering expression.

"O I'm sure we're about to find out," replied Raklen instead. "Correct little *Wraithling?"*

Loewen stared daggers at the Mortlake noble and then looked to Thesden. The rat upon her arm hissed at Raklen, presumably sensing the enmity it's mistress had for the noble. She needed Raklen for her father's sake but couldn't give a damn about the man. Loewen stuck out her tongue to lick her top lip and swayed provocatively as she re-adjusted her posture, pouted and sub-consciously began to caress her chin and lower neck.

Thesden smiled and stood casually, hands together un-threatingly. He eyed the girl's barely covered form up and down - it was certainly a sexier, if less practical, garment. Loewen arched her eyebrows as she regarded him, folding her arms so they accentuated her breasts. It was then Thesden realised she was eyeing *him* up. She smiled again, innocently playing with a fastening ribbon on her negligée style robe. Her eyes glittered with mischief and then she waved her hand dismissively at him, giggling with amusement. Thesden cocked his head to one side, curious at her taunt.

Loewen turned back to Gam, smiling wickedly; she seemed to be taking great delight in reveling in tormenting the Friar.

"I have been searching for my father's capturer, Gam," she said, pointing a bony finger at Raklen without meeting his stare. "For some time now in fact, ever since I orchestrated his escape from the gallows at Cheth."

Gam's eyes narrowed at learning this, otherwise there was no response. Judging by Loewen's irritation she had been expecting more, so she continued.

"It had come to my attention that an old crew member of my father's had reported a sighting of the Mortlake whelp after he had gone into hiding down here in Barrowdale. I also learnt, coincidentally, that Tinhallow abbey was looking to re-establish the chapel at Frostcross and they were sending a young acolyte to assist the new chaplain. It was an opportunity I simply couldn't resist! I befriended the girl; a little innocent thing named Loewen and then followed her. When the time was right I jumped and murdered her and took her place."

The Wraith's daughter embellished on the grisly murder of the young Tinhallow novice to Gam, to rile him further. Flexing her fingers, as proud as a peacock, she went on, "I recognised Jonah on arrival the eve before the real Loewen's intended arrival. I threatened him and got the information that I needed but Jonah didn't know exactly where the Mortlake filth resided - just that he had seen him visiting Frostcross. I was concerned that Jonah's loyalty no longer sat with his former crewmates and I didn't want to risk him exposing me and blowing my so cleverly conceived cover, so I followed him and killed him. Know it that I have informed my father and that even now he moves to join me here," she paused. "Have you nothing to say mentor Gam? How I so deceived you, how I so fooled you! I played you for a dupe, and right under your very nose as investigator!" She cackled loudly, "truly, have you nothing to say?"

Raklen and Thesden braced themselves as several zombies ambled up but stopped at the perimeter of the lane, merely blocking escape routes. They slowly watched the scene, slowly watching Loewen with cold eyes and awaiting instructions.

Raklen raised an eyebrow and glanced to Gam, who then uttered, "ye do like the sound of your own voice little viper. Well, aye ye fooled me and I admit, fooled me good. I chose to look passed some of your strangeness, especially at the barrow and now I look back at all those tell-tale remarks or mistakes and its as plain as day to me – ye found what Jonah had marked on his little map, hadn't ye?"

Loewen looked smug, "O yes. But you don't know the half of it. You see, I did find Jonah's map - his little retirement project here - but he actually hid it in the tree before I caught up with him – as if that would impede me. I worked out the code but couldn't find anything in the barrow but thought that someone, someone possibly like a cultured monk, might where I had failed. So, I left Jonah's corpse in the barrow and returned to the scene to put back the parchment but I heard your incompetent self coming - not quite the sophisticated monk I would have expected - and in rushing, it fell amongst the roots and I had to hide."

"That's why I could not understand why the killer wouldn't have found the map simply lying among the roots! Ye returned it – I thought someone was watching me."

The girl laughed, "It was hilarious when you thought Mortlake was the killer! When I was with you in the barrow I inadvertently found the secret compartment – and you thought I had been scared by a spider! I went back that night and found the statue – I could not expose myself till I new what it was, so I stayed behind pretending to be ill whilst I studied it." she proceeded to spit a short sentence of abysmal sounding words and at last revealed a small statuette in her hands and held it up. The statue was nothing more than some non-descript carved, limbless torso, made of a polished black rock. However, as she held it aloft a strong feeling of nausea washed over the companions. Loewen wretched from the sickness involved from chanting such unholy words, especially from what was obviously some powerful, nefarious artifact. With those unholy words seeping out into the night like reaching tentacles of sonic power the groan of nightmares awakening rose to its resonant bidding. A cluster of zombies joined the ones already encircling the companions. Loewen composed herself.

"We will all wait here together until my father arrives and I have a whole inn full of wanna-be zombies neatly sealed inside behind m..me!" she coughed and then continued to hack until she spat a globule of blood and mucus at the ground.

"Ye are sick!" began Gam.

"In more ways than one…" said Raklen under his breath.

Gam continued, "I know of this ancient statue from a dream-like vision and I know that only young girls seem to be able to wield it – it belongs in the ground away from the likes of mortals!" exclaimed Gam. "I saw what it did to poor Jonah, it was hideous, unimaginable, evil. The statue makes ye sick doesn't it?"

The girl ignored the remark and laughed long and loud, "if I couldn't control it, then yes, but I have the will in which to do so and re-direct its power against others, to raise the corpses to do my bidding. It couldn't have worked out better! With this statue my father will truly be a pirate King, with Barrowdale as his kingdom – a port at the Howl of the Ocean! The Dale folk will become his undead minions, his crew, the legion of a nameless fear!" she composed herself and re-uttered, "the Wraith is on his way!"

Gam understood that she had used the statue and raised the dead farmer from the wagon accident; the other zombies must have been Dalesmen that had died recently or those who the devil's child had helped on their way. Gam also realised that she couldn't have found the secret passage in the barrow though – she wouldn't have been able to resist rubbing his face in that too.

"Why are you helping these low-life's Gam? They are nothing but peasants and degenerates down here," she hissed and gave him a cold, hard stare.

"We have a motto at Tinhallow, one that poor Loewen would have taught you given the chance. It goes like this; that which is hallowed, we shall sustain, that which is virtuous, we will shield, that which torments, we will annihilate, for our grave wrath, will fathom no bounds."

Then, as if on key, the door behind the imposter Loewen, suddenly resounded with a loud bang and something hard struck it from behind and forced it open. Before Loewen could react, a stout log - probably reclaimed from the fireplace - came down hard on the girl's head with a sharp crack. The rat launched itself from her shoulder only to be snatched out of the air by Raklen and drop-kicked it over the Inn's roof with a screech.

Gam gasped as the face of her attacker appeared in the doorway, and he exclaimed, "Grim!"

"Its Bane actually," said the dour dwarf, chewing on his pipe, "Now get in here quick!"

The three needed no further urging and filed in to the inn just managing to slam the door shut in the faces of the descending zombie horde, the unconscious Loewen upon Gam's shoulder.

"Just what on earth is going on?" asked an exasperated Raklen, hurrying to bar the door too.

"There's no time now," intoned Bane, barring the doors with Raklen and with the added assistance from a collection of exceedingly pale-faced patrons. The Inn door began to tremble from the undead trying to force it open. "We have a foe at the threshold!"

CHAPTER SIX

Back to the

29th Eve, Lunar Cycle of the Cursed Constellation, 1189 Winters.

The pain shot through her abdomen, sending her arms and legs into spasmic fits. She screamed. But no one heard.

Her brain sorted through the multiple signals it was receiving, the intense pain from her stomach, the agony of her arms involuntarily striking the knobbly tree roots underneath her, the warmth of her own blood seeping over her skin, the cold night air against her exposed flesh. The dampness of the leaves and foliage against her back, the dizziness, the taste of blood in her mouth... she screamed again. But no one heard.

She struggled to glance down but a hand appeared from somewhere low and cuffed her head back. She murmured in pain from the subsequent strike of her head against a root. The woman moaned in despair, groaned, cried and then finally yelled once more as the pain below began to consume her... she screamed yet again. But still, no one heard.

Something hit her in the face, something wet. It blinded her momentarily and stung her eyes. Her brain tried to comprehend the substance against her face in between the shooting pain wracking her body, the flood of sensations, feelings, emotions - the fear, anxiety, horror, shock. Memories invaded her mind, images from her childhood, important events in her young life - her first kiss, first love, first embarrassment. Her teenage years - drinking, laughing, making love, falling in love...

Terrific pain began to envelope her, she was still squealing, still sobbing, she was alone, cold. In between the agony, her mind raced with questions, who was she? What was her name? Simple questions that she could no longer answer. Why was she here? What was happening to her? *Why* her?

Random images began to emerge in her mind again - a handsome, kind, male face. A baby... A baby smiling, gurgling. Then the images were gone as abruptly as they had appeared and the agony sent her brain spiralling out of control until it focused back onto the wet substance on her face, it was blood and soft organ material - it was hers!

She screamed once more, her precious red life-force draining away, the sensations from her skin had now been replaced by a prickling, pins and needles numbness but soon that was gone too. She breathed rapidly and spat blood from her mouth that threatened to suffocate her. Her rapid breathing and heart pounding only quickened the blood pumping out of her... and the inevitable.

She went to shriek but only a soft murmur escaped - it was all she could manage. And again, no one heard.

All she could hear now was her slowing heartbeat and the sound of... chewing... slurping. She attempted to lift her head again to look below, it was so, so heavy and the trees bowing over her began to spin. Something smashed her head back again but the pain on impact no longer registered. Something was killing her, eating her even but then the revulsion and fear disappeared. The kind, male face appeared once more and the baby, the smiling baby. Was her brain seeking to comfort her with images of love and affection, as it's last gift as the end came, as it began to shut down - perhaps showing her the more important persons in her life? She could no longer remember the names but she somehow knew she should. Then the anguish was gone and she felt free, warmer and at ease. She no longer tried to struggle or scream; she was resolved in her fate, knowing what was to come...

Her brain offered the images of the handsome man and baby one last time and she focused on them. Across her bruised, bloodied and mud clad face a slight smile began to appear and that was the last thing her body did before it succumbed to the extreme, torturous punishment, and died.

Her heart stopped. The blood slowed. The body cooled.

The feeding, fur-coated creature - gorged at last - moved off into the tree line, darkness its ally.

***

"I cannot be sure darlin', I was in the wood shed." his face was etched with concern as the husband and farmer approached his scared wife in the kitchen area of their small, homely abode.

"It was a scream, a woman's scream, I'm sure of it Jacobus!" spoke his wife with grave concern as she fiddled anxiously with the drapes over the window.

"Could it have been one o' the swine or, or maybe young lambs?" Jacobus offered, reaching his wife's side at the window but staying ever so slightly behind her.

"Jacobus. I know what I heard!" repeated Mayam, impatience tinting her tone. She caught him stepping back - he knew what was to come. Mayam loved her husband dearly but Jacobus was very *sensitive*.

Jacobus glanced up at his wife as she turned to face him. 'Wait for it,' he thought. And then it came.

"You'll have to go out and look!"

Jacobus inwardly flinched, but eventually nodded in acceptance. And so it was with great intrepidation, a churning stomach and tightly grasped hay fork, that Jacobus stepped out into the cold night air from the safety of the stone cottage.

Mayam peaked out through the crack of the doorway after her husband, who cautiously stepped into the night, lantern raised high in one hand, hay-fork held in front with the other.

A scraping sound drew Mayam's attention upwards. Something was scratching at the shingles on the roof - a bird perhaps. She edged out of the doorway, straining to look up and over the eaves, whilst keeping one eye on Jacobus as he crossed the courtyard. The scraping sound drew lower as something moved down the shingles, fear began to pound in her chest, constrict her throat - was it a bird, a small animal, or something else? She flashed urgent eyes to her husband's back as he walked away from her, if she called out it would alert the thing above to her dangerously close presence. But her eyes didn't locate him. Jacobus was gone. Mayam allowed herself a quick breath of surprise. A brief feeling of annoyance fluttered through her head at the misfortune of her husband's disappearance, though that soon turned to puzzlement, reflecting on his sudden departure and then turned to fear as the scraping sound, once again, came foremost to mind.

She edged back inside, preparing to slam the door, throw the bolt and run to the back door and locate Jacobus. However, the steady, constant noise from above suddenly stopped and Mayam hesitated at the silence, not daring to move and make a sound. It suddenly occurred to her that this indeed could be a bird or small animal, yet, the more she reflected on it, the more she second-guessed herself. She had to trust her instincts - this surly wasn't a small animal. After hearing that terrified, blood-chilling woman's scream - nothing pleasant could come after that.

The irony of the thought briefly struck her as the thing from above landed in front of her. Indeed, nothing pleasant *could* come after that.

Her eyes took in three images before a scream released from her throat – Jacobus's bloodied severed head, a fur-clad claw and saliva-dripping, expectant fangs closing in on her.

Somehow she ducked and jaws snapped shut just to her right. Her mind blank - perhaps paralysed with fear - she fled from the scene but not into the cottage. She screamed for help not letting the futility of the call affect her, after all, their nearest neighbour was Danick and he lived in a small cottage close to the Meddle but that was still half a day's walk.

Mayam sprinted as fast as she could into the woodland. There was nothing but silence behind her but she dared not look back and risk losing her footing in the tree roots. Suddenly a rasping sound from somewhere above came to her ears and she knew what it was a moment before it hit her.

The creature - its snapping maw thoroughly etched in her mind - landed on her and pinned her to the ground. It was mix of wolf and human - bipedal and fur clad - enlarged canines sprouting from its saliva-dripping maw but it was the fetid stench of it's breath that caught in her throat and made her wretch, just as a burning sensation slashed across her lower abdomen.

Too weak to call out she was resigned to her fate. The next thing she heard were sudden footsteps, snapping twigs, a fearsome battle cry and the creature howling. She managed to glance up and saw that the wolf creature was staggering back, a long spear projecting from its side. She could see a glint of silver shining from the front of the creature and realised it was the spear's tip which had penetrated all the way through. Just before she lost consciousness she recognised the long matted, blond hair tumbling under a worn silver helm, dirty yet functional chainmail and a flapping jade cloak.

"Danick," she whispered in relief, before the darkness took her forever.

The wild man from Oscaig knew that evil had begun to stir in Barrowdale. He had seen it from his long boat whilst fishing off the point. A pack of ghoulish creatures hunting like hyenas along the coast. He had fought his way to his cottage to secure the weapons and armour from his early days as an explorer. Realising he needed to warn the unsuspecting folk of Barrowdale, he had powered on, leaving his precious last batch of peat-smoked salmon to rot.

Danick stroked his beard and shook his head, staring down at the woman's body through the goggle like visor on his helm. Mayam, bless her, didn't have a chance. He knew, if he was to warn other Dale folk before they perished he had to press on, and, as far as he knew, he was the only being out here who knew the way through Barrowdale's peat bog, known locally as the Meddle. If he succeeded unhindered he would strike out on the main track to Frostcross adjacent to Iron Peak.

Relinquishing the broken speak for his axe and checking the harness on his shield, he nodded respectfully toward Mayam's body and uttered a quiet line to whatever god chose to listen.

"This day we see who will triumph, creature or man. Let them come to me and let the gods decide." With that, the Norseman from Oscaig took off at a trot.

After a short while he had entered the edge of the marshy Meddle and for the last mile, he was certain he was being followed. Careful to try and mask his passage he soon came across two mounds of bones. Then, stretching off in the distance to his left and right were skulls hanging from poles staked into the ground like a crudely made fence. Parts of skeletons hung from now dead rotting trees, twisted in agonising forms. An odour of rotting meat pervaded and the flies were growing thick. He could make out small creatures scurrying through the rancid scene, making agod awful noise. A large, slick, black snake brushed passed his feet – setting them faster into motion. Danick hurriedly moved off, wanting to get as much distance between him and this place before the deep dark of nightfall.

Eventually the evening skies began to settle in, darker clouds loomed up covering the moon. Danick came to a small hill with trees on top and going down one side. With the amount of shrubbery surrounding the scattered trees, it made for a very sheltered spot. He decided this would make a reasonable place to spend a few hours to sleep.

After a short meal of spiced potatoes and fish, the wilderness warrior found a spot between a tree and bush which had a carpet of ferns. He set a ring of dried sticks - about ten meters from him - in a circle and settled down inside it for the night. Pulling his thick cloak around him, within moments he was lightly dozing, with trusted axe in hand.

The clouds parted, revealing the moon, silhouetting an owl in the pale light. The bird of prey scanned over the area, searching with its keen eyes for movement that could lead to its supper. The keen-eyed bird was feeding later than normal as the wildlife had been disturbed by a man who had the cheek to spend the night under his tree. The owl kept a constant vigil and noticed a disturbance amongst the bushes around the furthest tree. Through the blackness came the sound of tortured cries.

The bird of prey froze, staring at the intrusion, it hooted and took comfort by it's own call. A light fog closed in and rolled around the trunks of the trees. The wind did not increase but a stench drifted in, growing in intensity and it carried now the wails of the unknown, moving towards the lone tree. The owl sensed movement from the man and realised that he also could make out the shapes moving towards them.

Danick awoke to hear a rustle in the bushes at the edge of the trees and the smell of dead flesh. With it came a fog, creeping up, winding around the leafy trees, reaching out further. An owl hooted above him in the tree, then took to the sky, leaving this region. Danick acknowledged it was time to leave too; as the moon went in and the countryside fell into darkness. Suddenly, there was movement to his right, accompanied by a soft grunt. The short hairs rose across the back of Danick's neck and along his forearms. He stared into the darkness probing the blackness, not daring to even exhale. Then he heard a distant snarling and the bile rose in his throat. Danick tried to locate the direction of the sound but the gloom, allied to the Meddle's dips and folds in the ground, made it difficult to pinpoint the exact bearing. A snarl suddenly came to his ears from close by, there was no doubt to him that something was moving towards him, drawing inexorably closer with each ragged breath.

Quietly and cautiously, Danick moved away from the danger. Carefully, he stepped over his ring of dried wood and moved off. He picked up his pace, arriving at a small ford. He scrambled to the top and looked around, scanning to see what and how many creatures confronted him. Danick's face visibly paled and his mouth dropped in dismay. The vast area of ground behind him seemed to writhe and wail with the walking dead.

Danick could not guess how many were out there, maybe hundreds. The undead line stretched far off to each side, a line made up of shambling zombies, who had pulled themselves up from the clinging mud - victims of a battle that none now remembered. Glowing pearlescent white spirits drifted over the bog, their forms shimmering, distorting, discordant wails carried to Danick'e ears. He turned and jumped, splashing into the ford, he waded to the far bank, scrambled up it and fled as fast as he could into the night. The moon came out, transforming the fog into a ghostly silver blanket and revealing the pressing danger. Now with movement visible on three sides, Danick ran as fast as he could. A ghoul sniffed at the air, hunting him with sunken, hollow eyes and grasped to snag him with sharp talons and he knocked it aside with a great sweep of his weapon.

Danick knew that the night had many hours left and even the dawn did not guarantee an end to the pursuit.

A smaller group, consisting of about twenty to thirty zombies, ghouls and sea-spectres - still in their phantasmal pirate garb - had broken away from the vast tide of pursuing undead.

Danick could run no further. Close to complete exhaustion, he decided to stand and fight, to die with honour, rather than to be trampled down like some rat, in the lonely bogs. The thought of becoming one of these damned creatures filled him with dread but also the determination to fight and be victorious was stronger than ever.

Thunder boomed in the sky, lightning flashed, the abrupt light picked out two zombies who loomed up blocking his way; their open mouths and rotting features shuddering with excitement at the prospect of carnage. Danick gave it to them. He charged, snarling in rage and chanting his favourite war song Danick struck.

"The winding path, over roots of old..."

His first blow cut through one of the zombies splitting its stomach open and sending foul stinking, rotting intestines to the ground. He ran by, letting the axe's momentum continue to shred the bunched undead. They groaned, falling to the ground, claw-like hands raining around the Norseman as he charged through. Danick rushed up a small hill; the stubborn zombies close in pursuit with more of their wretched kin in tow.

"...Walking in further favour the bold..."

Danick hurried up the hill. Finally he reached the top, turned and readied himself for the onslaught - holding his shield high, axe slowly swinging in menacing circles. Then they were on him.

"...A dance of green, those eyes unseen..."

Luckily, the emaciated ghouls began to show caution, pushing at each other so only a handful attacked at once.

"...On that trek of ages with warriors and sages..."

Danick kicked the first zombie, sending it back down the hill taking another with it.

"...A watchful line with wary swords drawn..."

Before he could catch his breath, another had taken its place.

"...The attack comes in hours, near dawn..."

Danick slashed out, cutting deep into a zombie; before he pulled out his axe, bashed it back with his shield and withdrew and buried his axe violently into the head of another zombie.

"...Where the trees dipped low, and the light did not go..."

The undead slumped down the slope. The stink was overpowering.

"...The savages struck with merciless speed..."

He turned, swinging his axe around his head, keeping the struggling ghouls and zombies from coming up behind him.

"...The horsemen charged, their spear-pennants whipped..."

Rusty weapons and filthy hands swung at him, shredding his already torn clothes, occasionally cutting him with their wild swings.

"...As they drew close, their spears dipped..."

He swung his axe, driving it deep into a ghoul, foul blood sprayed over Danick as he pushed the axe home, nearly cleaving it in two.

"...the release and strum of arrows of fire..."

He wrenched his axe free and kicked the ghoul down the hill.

"...Foes' foul lives were taken so dire..."

Out of the corner of his eye, Danick saw a zombie shambling toward him from the side. He withdrew a small throwing axe and hurled it expertly at the creature.

"...Warrior's assailed, axes-a-spinning..."

The axe flew end over end and buried into the zombies neck, cleaving its chin and spraying the pack with black, pungent liquid.

"...With cries of the dead, their swords were winning..."

Danick turned in time to meet another, he brought his axe down hard and cut off a newly risen zombie's arm. It landed at Danick's feet; he kicked it into a throng of thin-limbed ghouls, who dived to feast on the tasty arm.

"...priests prayed aloud to heal the pained..."

A ghoul lashed out at the warrior and he reacted to the assault with a counter attack of unmatched fury.

"...Though brave men fell, freedom was gained..."

Danick stabbed upwards with his axe into its stomach and pulled up hard. The axe sliced through the ghoul's chest; it cried out in agony as it's rib cage splintered under the strength of the axe.

"...Have at them, and drive them back, let their blood pave our way to victory..."

Danick spun around to face another flesh-hungry ghoul; the wilderness warrior's axe cut in cleanly, slicing into the ghoul's neck and followed through, beheading the vulgar creature.

"...That ringing of steel, shouts of the brave..."

Several of the starving ghouls grappled with their headless kin and began to feed.

Danick had a thought. He launched at several zombies, swinging his axe at head height. The walking dead fell, having received unrecoverable head wounds. The remaining ghouls dived onto the thrashing bodies, beginning to feed on each other, rather than risk the trial of the combat.

With the ghoul's in a feeding frenzy and distracted, Danick ran down the hill toward the river but his foot slipped and he swore as he started to slide in the mud, lose his balance and tumble down.

Danick rolled into a dyke. It stretched away from him, disappearing into the wetlands like a slow-worm into the gorse. The smell from the bottom of the ditch was foul; a pungent, nostril-pinching mix of peat and stagnant water. There was another strong odour too. Danick could make out a heaped shape lying close; the remains of one of the ghouls, and it was staring at him. Some spark of life glinted from its evil eyes and Danick had no choice but to quickly sink his axe into its head before it could cry out. He wondered how long the creature would have taken to die if left alone? He swatted away the mosquitoes and didn't care. With a burst of energy he flung himself over the bank and into the freezing waters of the Meddle – where wading through the murky water would confuse the ghouls and zombies. It was time to put this place and the supernatural spectres behind him.

He swam through the water, until he was in the centre of the river and only then did he glance back. The zombies shambled menacingly around the bank, dragging their twisted bodies with them, their eyes staring vacantly upward. One had even accidentally waded out into the river. The ghouls lurked around a small patch of tangled, twisted trees, nervously eyeing the arriving spirit host. Bestial howls filled the night sky - eyes a baleful red glow of hatred and malice. Careful not to reveal his presence, Danick half-swam, half-waded, further upstream.

Soon the river grew very deep and he reached for a log. He hauled his body on top the best he could and used his hands to paddle the log into motion, he lay still as he drifted off further. He could see the various forms of walking dead searching for him on the bank, trying to locate his scent, the occasional fight breaking out between frustrated ghouls. Further Danick floated off, out, into the still waters.

Danick was exhausted yet quite content. Letting the log carry him away, he grew more comfortable with the eerie hush of the Meddle. Using a dagger he pried a leach from his arm and tossed it casually back into the bog, ignoring the bleeding wound.

Danick splashed through the water to the bank, and climbed up, the weight of his chainmail beginning to tell. The sun was beginning to rise and the fog, to dissipate. He stumbled through the bent and twisted tree roots and sat on an old stump, exhausted. He only dared a few ten breaths of rest before skulking swamp creatures stirred from their dark caves, located his scent and hunted for food. In his mind's eye he saw the ghouls, eyes bright – just like that one in the ditch – their tongues slavering, straining to taste his flesh. Noon brought him to a vague trail which started to climb along the bare shoulders of brown, sere hills. Danick looked to the west and the scattering of small grey peaks, some of the highest prominences to be found amongst the barrow-downs and it's tallest - the claw-like, lone mount of Iron Peak. He could also see trees in the distance; not twisted swamp trees but fir trees, the edge of a thick wood and the lone mount beyond. He began to jog, finally on firm ground.

Danick picked up his pace as he suddenly heard footsteps behind him, coming faster and faster. Danick began to run at full speed, the forest getting closer with every step. A slavering ghoul stepped out from the bushes and knocked Danick off his feet, he landed hard, hitting his head against a fallen tree. He picked himself up but was pushed down again by the creature; he spun on his back and lashed out with his axe, which cut into the ghoul's calf. The creature lost its balance and also fell. Danick hacked at the fallen undead with his axe, putting his foot on it's neck, holding it down and hacking it repeatedly in the face, inflicting horrific wounds. The ghoul wailed, revealing their position to the rest of its frenzied kin. Danick sprang up, running as fast as he could. He stumbled, dizziness creeping over him from his head wound.

The forest was close and he couldn't give up now, not when he had come so far. A ghoul sprang at Danick from behind, knocking him down. He wriggled, trying to free himself but was pinned - all thoughts of escape stifled. He could not pull his axe free, so, in desperation, with his free hand he punched the vile creature in the face. It twisted on top of him allowing the release of his axe with which he struck the undead. The axe cleaved down its face, slicing off about a third of it, foul stinking blood saturated Danick. He pulled himself free of the ghoul and sank his axe into it. As he rose, a lone zombie shambled out of the gloom, the pestilential creature reached out with sharp, disease-ridden nails to rake him, but its slow demeanour could not catch the Norseman and furiously spinning his axe, made short work of its miserable existence.

Leaving it in a crumpled, steaming heap; it's dissolving organs sending putrid gases into the air.

Shaking his head to clear the wooly sensation, he jogged across the grassy plains glad for it to be firm under foot. Relief flowed through him as Iron Peak loomed up above him.

"Danick, hold!" came a voice to his left. Instinctively, the warrior raised his trusted axe but then paused. A dwarf he recognised was bent over the corpse of a young girl dressed in the remnants of a brown acolyte's robe. With a furrowed brow he wandered over to the scene.

***

The present;

30th Eve, Lunar Cycle of the Cursed Constellation, 1189 Winters.

The Fool's Nook door thundered and shook with the strain of so many undead creatures trying to force entry. Thick dust slipped from the ledge above the door as it bucked from the pounding and a grating noise that could only be fingernails, scratched furiously on the thick timber.

"One thing I just couldn't stomach living here; all the damn undead!" exclaimed Bardon, abruptly. Gutiso nodded in agreement.

Gam recoiled and looked quite shocked, "I never dared to mention the ghosts, sea spectres or worse I came to witness - afraid of scaring ye locals. And now ye tell me this! Well I'll be a baboon's burgundy bum - Ye knew all along?"

Bardon looked at him expressionless.

"No wonder I found everything for a slayer's kit in Gutiso's store!" cried Gam as the door continued to rattle on its hinges.

By this time Gutiso, Ervan and Tith were bracing the door but continued to look back at the Friar - a stunned look upon their faces as he ranted away, seemingly unconcerned at the foul creatures trying to gain access.

"It just needs some whoreson-of-a-gull to shat upon mi shiny noggin' to make this day complete!" hollered Gam, face reddening. Bardon slipped away through a doorway behind the bar.

"Fine time to go losing it!" shouted Tith, as she shuddered from the clattering door and watched Bardon leave, "when I said to..." she stopped mid-sentence as the beastly beings who were trying to force entry suddenly stopped. The door became silent and still. They all stared on. Long moments passed.

Gutiso looked back to the others, shrugged his shoulders and gently pressed his ear to the door listening for the tell-tale groans.

"I think they've gone," he said optimistically. "If..." he got no further as the door thundered and shook, knocking Gutiso's head in the process and making all those staring jump considerably.

"We're all doomed!" screamed Tith, grabbing hold of Gam's considerable girth and peeking around his belly at the door.

"No we're not!" announced Raklen, as he strode in from the door behind the bar - he was carrying his basket-hilted, ornate sword and a long-bladed dagger. Bardon appeared from behind him, "If they're willin' to 'elp us, we should be willin' to 'elp ourselves. I 'ave a stash o' weapons I keep in the basement. Here." The Innkeeper started to hand them out to his regulars.

"Agreed," came a voice, entering through the doorway at that particular point.

"Thesden - what have ye found?" asked Gam, pushing Tith into Gutiso's arms. Thesden was armoured in a hotchpotch of pieces - leather bracers, a chain mail coif and an ill-fitting piece of ring mail hung around his midriff. He rested a large, two-handed war hammer, on his shoulder.

"This suit you Tith?" he mused handing the hammer over. Tith yelped and nearly dropped it; the others chuckled lightly, glad for a lighter moment - no matter how brief - as the door then thundered again.

"Its gonna give!" shouted Gutiso, desperately taking an old short sword from Bardon and holding it out in front of him - his lack of skill with an edged weapon was already quite obvious.

"No," continued Tith, offering the hammer's shaft back to Thesden, as the hammer head was too heavy for her to lift from the floor. "I'll use this!" she announced, relieving Thesden of his favoured glaive. He sighed but let her take his weapon all the same.

"...I'm serious!" frantically shouted Gutiso, the sword visibly trembling in his weedy arms, "the door is going to g..give!"

"I'll be right wif you!" shouted Bardon, reaching under the bar; the burly Innkeeper emerged with a hefty axe and an ancient helmet, belonging to his grandpappy which he announced proudly. Bardon reached the door to stand alongside Gam, Raklen and Thesden just as the wooden door gave way.

The entrance exploded, sending timber pieces and splinters in all directions. The candles sputtered in their wall sconces and blew out, a disgusting smell infused. A blood curdling scream followed as a zombie who led the assault was decapitated by a well aimed strike from a prepared Raklen. In the following confusion and settling dust, Thesden ran forward to meet the vile undead attackers. He raised the war hammer and brought it down fiercely on the next zombie as it forced its way through the opening, over the twitching form of its kin. It's neck was driven down into its body with a sickening snap. Two corpses now piled in the doorway.

As one, a shambling cluster of undead streamed into the inn. The first of the zombies was a twisted display of undeath; the once human visage was swollen, stretched and hung in tatters revealing the glistening bone underneath. Many barbed, small tentacles - like coiling snakes - appeared from deep within the re-animated corpse to dance around it's head, eager to rip into the living. The two undead monstrosities next in line - as they fought to get passed each other in the confines of the doorway - were the human-like zombies Gam had already faced – they just appeared as reanimated corpses. The next had an unnaturally large mouth which was snapping with sharp, needle teeth, determined to forcibly bury them into it's prey. It focused on Tith, who screamed when she comprehended its motive and, still screaming, fled like a young hare for the cover of the bar.

Gam joined Raklen and Thesden's assail, just as he brought his hammer down, crushing needle-teeth to the ground. Bardon, likewise, faced another zombie with his axe. He unleashed at it with furious rage. Strike after strike sent the creature reeling. He lunged out, severing a hand from one of the zombies and spun awkwardly, losing his helmet. The innkeeper reached out to steady himself, accidentally grabbing the nearest, shambling monstrosity. The undead was surprised by the move, overbalanced and faltered. It went for Bardon's axe, stopping the innkeeper from using it; Bardon, unflinching, landed a head-butt between its cruel, unfeeling eyes, sending it down to the stone floor. Ervan slipped in from behind and brought a heavy statue - which he had claimed from a plinth in the corner - upon its head, again and again. The zombie shuddered from the fatal wounds and instinctively its arm shot out, pulling one of the cheerfully burning lanterns down from it position on the stand. It would not have normally been a concern except that it landed on a fallen tapestry and coupled with the spilled liquors lying in small puddles here and there, caught alight with furious speed. Dancing flames and billowing smoke erupted in all directions before Ervan could even cry a warning.

Several skulking zombies, deciding whether or not to join the battle as the flames took effect, edged in more cautiously. Tith began screaming and crying out to the heroes in the doorway, as she cowered under the bar. More tapestries and even the furniture began to catch alight, turning the scene into some horrific firework display gone wrong. Gam's eyes were wide and staring at the speed of the rolling flames - not as wide as Bardon's however.

"We need to move out and away from the inn!" shouted Gam, observing the vile vista, as further screams began to echo around the room.

Raklen, Bane and Thesden nodded to each other and worked their weapons together, sending sharp blades and bludgeoning strikes dancing into the zombies, cutting them to ribbons with skillful swordplay and competent clouts.

A terrified scream startled Gam, as a Fisherman in trying to help their cause was plucked from the scrum and dragged backward through the air into the mass of zombies. A fountain of crimson gushed high into the air, until the screaming stopped.

Men were simply not used to fighting such despicable creatures and none should have to be, Gam just hoped the others did not panic and flee into the night where they would be hunted as prey and killed. They needed to stay together - but they needed to get out.

"We can't hold them off forever or stay here any longer - we must get away!" he called out, bringing his hammer down and crushing another zombie to the ground. The others grunted in agreement, Bardon likewise as he faced another fell zombie, loose skin hanging off its bones. He saw the still body of one of his tavern-girls and unleashed at the zombie with furious rage.

Thesden went to grab the Innkeeper as the others backed away from the door, "it's far from over Bardon. Nothing we can do though will stop the inevitable! The Fool's Nook is coming down around our very ears!"

Bardon snapped out of his fury and nodded quickly, "there's anuver door out this way - its be'ind a 'edge in the courtyard with Gut's barn, only thee and me use it."

Gam remembered seeing the courtyard from his room above. With renewed vigour boosting all those with him, they surged around the bar in his wake as zombies were crushed by falling timbers and clumps of masonry, as the flames took effect.

An urgent, warning call from Gam came too late as a Crofter span from an attack behind. The unfortunate man cried out and span around yet again - involuntarily, deep cuts marring his chest and stomach. Gam went to catch him but he had lifted the unconscious Loewen to his shoulder and was unable to reach him with the extra burden. He countered a reaching zombie arm with his hammer, and the falling timbers did the rest. The zombie disappeared through the burning wooden floor. Gam shouted for help but the Crofter's body was snagged and taken into the burning depths with the zombie. He had no choice but to follow after his companions as they disappeared from the burning taproom and followed Bardon on his escape route.

Gam caught up with Bane as the dwarf in turn was tagging along after the rest of the group as they made their way out of the inn, across a small courtyard and - thanks to Gutiso - disappeared inside his barn on the opposite side.

"How did ye know about Loewen Bane?" the Friar asked, indicating the girl on his shoulder. The dwarf acknowledged the girl with his squinting eyes as they continued to hurry on.

"I found a girl's body dumped off the track near where I live at Iron Peak. She was wearing the robes of Tinhallow, yet she had been dead for a while. Nasty works a foot I thought and drew this conclusion."

Bane described the girl at Gam's beckoning and then Gam realised that he knew her, or at least of sorts. "It had been this girl's spirit that I had encountered on the trail outside of Frostcross not long after my arrival." He shook his head sadly. Bane took the cue and continued, "I revealed my discovery to Danick and sent him with his knowledge of the Meddle to seek help from Tinhallow, raise the Militia and t'come straight here!"

"Truly?" asked Gam urgently, stopping the dwarf by grappling his shoulder in order to judge those heavy set eyes. "By the beard of mi mother, I swear it true!"

Gam nodded his head after the others who were disappearing through the other side of the barn and beckoned Bane on, smiling faintly. The barn was empty and all the horses had long since bolted. Gutiso led them to his store where they quickly grabbed supplies, weapons and such like, whilst Raklen and Gam stood watch.

"How did you know about the statue Gam and what that damned girl was doing?" asked Raklen, staring intently across the street at the burning Inn as he uttered his question.

"Well, it's a strange one, but I had some kind of dream, nightmare even - it was, odd. I'd visited the barrow twice in trying to discern what was lying within. Jonah had left a map y'see but apparently Loewen had discovered it in secret before I. Now that we have retaken this cursed statue we must bury it at Iron peak, fore that is where it ended in my dream. Iron Peak *must* be its final resting place, to be buried and forgotten. It appears to only work for children - girls in fact. Why? I do not know." Gam remembered how he had witnessed no change from the artifact or the father's behavior whilst the prehistoric man possessed it in the dream. It was only when the daughter received it and - unlike Loewen - failed to understand or wield it correctly, did it flare into life. He turned to face Raklen, his eyes reflecting the writhing orange of the blazing building. "I can only presume the ancient people who formed the barrows around these parts had found it, learnt its evil and decided to hide it safely away with their deceased leader once and for all. I do not understand its properties and I'm not sure I want to." Gam slipped the Wraith's daughter off his shoulder and wrapped a further layer of material around the statue as it sat snuggly in his pack.

"I can feel its heaviness - something supernatural and sinister. It pulses like a heartbeat that I can feel..."

"Even now?" Raklen asked, tearing his eyes from the lane also in order to regard Gam.

"Even now," the Friar intoned somberly. "I will pass it to Bane where he can arrange to send it deep into the earth under Iron Peak."

Raklen nodded in agreement and then directly turned back to the street, "Can you hear that?" he urgently asked.

"Unfortunately, I can. It's the undead - they're coming!" stated Gam. Raklen moved to the door and shouted for the others. They all filed out of the store like bees escaping a smoking hive and Gam led them away and behind the store. He led them, knowing that he had left Loewen lying on the porch of the store and without the statue, he doubted she could control the zombies - doubted she would survive. Shame.

Gam guided the rag-tag group up into the meadow, just as he and Loewen originally had when setting off for Scarpel Rock for the first time. Recalling that morning had suddenly given Gam a cunning idea.

"Where are we goin'?" demanded Bardon, as they followed Gam across the dark downs. "We'll be caught upon the hills like rats in a trap and cut down!"

"I tell ye we will not," began Gam, taking a small wooden torch from Tith and lighting it with flint and tinder when he was happy to be out of eye shot of Frostcross. He handed the enlightening beacon to Tith and smiled at the woman, though still addressing Bardon, the others looked on curiously. "If ye trust me, then follow me and I will lead us to a secret that Barrowdale herself only knows - a passage to the sea and a sea-worthy schooner moored for our grace and pleasure," he addressed the others. "Danick alerts the militia to our plight and will bring down a force of Chandorians to the area, like a cleansing wave. We just need to stay clear and absent till their arrival." At the mention of the militia, a ripple of relief passed through the frightened group of Frostcross folk drawn around him. Gam smiled and nodded to Raklen, "Aye, we'll all be fine, if we just keep going. Those zombies will smell us out for sure and keep coming after us like an unrelenting pack of wolves. Are ye with me?"

Gam knew he couldn't answer all the questions that would surely be aimed at him but looking into the eyes so intent upon him, it was obvious they didn't want to know the answers - they didn't want to address any faults in a plan. Just that there was a plan and it offered a safe way out. It offered hope.

Bardon began to hum a low note, then another, a little higher in pitch. He looked to Gam, nodded and then to the others, blossoming into a tune. It was recognisable to all but Gam, a legendary Dale song of inspiring content. The others, one by one, joined with Gam. A few even broke into proud smiles.

Ye breathe the air of nature's wealth,
green pastures, dales, life's sacred health,
the realm we love, this Barrowdale soil,
under-threat so foul, our mortal toil.

But, the nigh-times pass,
and the daylight lasts,
O, shivers gone,
orange orb - to rise up from.

Montasp's peaks so wide,
enlightens the land south of Chandorian's stride,
from four-walled city spires,
wooded hills, to marsh and mires.

The cost may be steep,
but rewards of peace, we gladly reap,
to stay our homes,
our castled homes.

And step up to, defend this land of old,
Dale men we, were never a man so bold.

Gam enthusiastically took point with Raklen and led, whilst Bane and Thesden took rear guard.

By Jove, he would lead them to the Oakstone barrow, through its hidden belly and to the safety of the moored schooner beyond, as if the very gods were at their backs.

The hair stood to attention on the nape of his neck as he discerned a howl of pleasure from some way off in the direction of Frostcross. The palms of his hands went clammy, a chill gripped at his heart. Gam took it as a sign that the undead monstrosities had picked up their scent and now unquestionably pursued them across the wind-swept downs. He began to murmur the very dale song that raised the ailing spirits of those he escorted and to settle his own plan-nagging demons.

***

With darkened splendour, pale and gaunt, how she sees her zombie horde jaunt. The stench of death, the decaying tide, limbs rotting away, skin hanging like hide.

From the devil whore's host, her foes dare run and stray. Their slaughter is demanded and demanded without delay...

Thus so, the cruel girl laughs with pleasure and surprise, "Daddy!"

CHAPTER SEVEN

30th and last night,

Lunar Cycle of the Cursed Constellation, 1189 Winters.

The slap of the waves against the schooner's hull was drowned by the howl of the ocean as it swept up and pounded the rolling coastline.

A queasy Gam peered down at the waves, black tipped and pearl like in the moonlight, reflecting on his jammy luck to have successfully led the group through the passage to the schooner. Even with the savage howls of the walking dead behind, they had embarked without hindrance and made their escape. Now, if he could only escape this sea-sickness to boot, he would be a jolly and thankful friar indeed.

Relieved of his watch at the wheel by Thesden - where he had been every bit as useless as he had expected, he now strolled carefully down the deck, heading for the bow. He'd cleared the cabin housing when the schooner's sails were hoisted by Ervan and Bardon and suddenly the wind caught its sails and the vessel leapt forward.

Gam cursed and just managed to stifle the sound. He was flung against the bale lashed to the railing. His desperately groping fingers tangled in the lashings. Drawing a deep breath, he hauled himself up.

Immediately he'd regained his feet, he heard an almighty crack, like a tree branch snapping.

"Gam, duck!"

He reacted more to Raklen's tone than the words, but duck he did. The boom went sailing passed, level with where his head had been only moments before. Gam stared at the long pole swinging outward over the waves, a rope dangling behind it. Trying to lend a hand in view of his blunder, he went to assist and grabbed the rope. Instantly, he realised his mistake. The sudden tug on his arms was horrendous and then he was being hauled in the wake of the boom, the wind filling the sail and causing the heavily laden schooner to list to the starboard. Gam shouted a curse, not muffling it this time, and looked down at the black waves, remembering he couldn't swim.

His belly hit the bale and just when he thought he had doomed them all, Raklen and Thesden were there adding their weight to his and hauling on the rope. The boom swung back and they balanced the wind in the sail. The schooner raced forward and Raklen wound the rope around the rail.

"That should do it. Stay on this heading and we will soon clear the rocks and the point beyond. Let us get a good look into the Shoremeet and see what we can see, hey?"

Eventually they cleared the dangerous rocks and whirlpools that all fisherman new well to avoid, and the narrow body of water stretching to the Shoremeet came into view. The tide was flowing in fast, eating away the beach. On their right, the cliff swept up to a rocky out-crop, then fell to a rock strewn point with three tall standing stones projecting from it's face. They were known locally as the Twilight Maidens, and if one was to glance up from their tips you could follow a line all the way to the hill where the chapel dwelt. Gam was pleased not to see any sign that the inn was still burning, he would have expected to be viewing an orange glow in the valley and billowing smoke for that matter. But there was nothing.

The surf ran high at this rocky tip; the crash of waves cloaked the scene in noise. As they all ardently watched at the Schooner's hand rail, a light drizzle started to fall and a mist began to form near the point. The fog draped the gently sloping and rugged landscape, floating spectrally along atop the rolling water.

The clamour of steel on steel somewhere inland came to the Dalesmen's ears as they crowded the rail. They looked to Gam for an explanation on the discordant sound of battle. Dark clouds scudded before the moon and it was a ten-breath till he could look for answers in the fitful light but as the clouds cleared they could all see for themselves.

It was hard to make out but a banner held aloft above a contingent of men was unmistakeable - it was the Mortlake banner and thusly in the shape of a castle.

"Its the Chandorian Militia!" announced Thesden, standing on tip toes a mere moment before Gam exclaimed the same.

"Aye, thank goodness, but how are they here so damn quick!" asked Gutiso joining them at the rails.

"Nay sure, but it must be the Wraith they're locked in combat with," said Gam shaking his head. He looked to Raklen.

"I concur," the noble responded and then smiled. "You don't even need to ask. We *must* aid them."

"I'm in too!" agreed Thesden, the ex-soldier, and clasped Gam and Raklen by their shoulders. Gam responded with a confident smile but cautiously looked to the others, the likes of Ervan, Gutiso, Tith even.

"One of us will have to stay with the schooner and remain out at sea until its safe, or, so they can at least make their escape if our cause is lost."

"Where is Bane?" asked Thesden abruptly and looked around for the grim dwarf, "come to think of it, I haven't seen him since we've been on board!"

Raklen chuckled, "he cowers in the cabin. Dwarfs and water don't mix!"

A groaning sound echoed from the cabin followed by wretching and a throaty curse.

"Its settled then," said Thesden with a chortle. "*He* should stay!"

"That's cruel," replied Raklen. "But amusing, I vote for Bane to stay too! He does guard the statue and we certainly do not want to risk that falling into the Wraith's dirty mitts!"

"Aye, it makes sense," said Gam. "But for goodness sake though, don't tell 'im till we've left. He'll be hopping mad!"

Raklen and Thesden left the handrail to prepare for their departure but Gam stayed put, his hands fixed to the rail. The sight of the beach was far more welcome than the rocks.

Gam saw Thesden wave as they neared the shallow water. "Untie the rope and let it slowly!" he called lightly. Gam did as he was told, wary of the wind-whipped sail. The boom swung away but the wheel was also swung by Thesden. The schooner slewed and slowed as the wind emptied from the sail. The boom swung inward. Gam had seen the boom returning but judged it erroneously; fortunately, he felt abrupt hands on his shoulders.

The deck was hard and uncomfortable, but it was doubtless better than a broken head. He nodded his thanks to Raklen and noticed Tith at the stern stifle a giggle. For the first time since entering the schooner he also noted Gutiso's face and the youthful, happy look across his features - apparently the adventure and break from his usual routine was doing him some good as well.

Gam, Raklen and Thesden slipped over the side of the schooner, gently bobbing on the shallow swell and waded to shore. The water was cold and Gam moved quickly through the waves and slowly made his way out of the surf as fitful clouds had found the moon yet again. Once on the beach they quickly but cautiously headed for the battle, merely dark blotches on the horizon.

As they moved off, Gam risked a quick glance back to the schooner as it struggled back out though the surf. Turning back, the ground ahead disappeared into blackness as the clouds cleared and then once again loomed over the moon.

It was dim and dark on the sands. The surf boomed; the crash of waves and the slurping suck of the tide filled Gam's ears. Moisture from the sea air had begun to soak his robe and with his already dripping-wet breeches, added to his discomfort. Suddenly, a muffled shout reached him, followed by a second - gruff voices barely audible above the surf, and as the moon escaped the clouds, he realised the battle was closer than he had originally thought.

The three companions jogged effortlessly up the beach as the clamour of battle on the grasslands beyond came to their ears all at once. The clang of steel, the savage cheers of the triumphant, the death wails of the unfortunates. Man slaughtered man, the brutality and the savagery - it made the battle all too frightfully real and true.

The moon sailed free and Gam saw the pirates quite easily now and watched with fascination as the mist crept in further around them and sought the land with its white, reaching tendrils. For at least a forty-breath, as his chest rose and fell, Gam watched. If he, Raklen and Thesden were going to lend a hand, they couldn't afford to be seen approaching - the clouds were unreliable but fortunately this mist would serve them well.

It appeared that the contingent of Chandorian Militia were grouped around their standard and holding their own against the mass of pirates and what looked like the gangly forms of a few ratmen. What interested the three more were a small group, set slightly further off, overseeing the battle. A tall silhouette and a smaller one - Gam was absolute when he branded them with curses as the Wraith and Loewen. It wasn't lost on the noble and farmer that only a few pirate bodyguards stood with them, two of which had broken away and were moving nearby.

Raklen and Thesden looked to each other and then to Gam, he nodded solemnly. The two men strode forward, glaive in one practiced hand, a sword in the others.

Two pirates moved out of the gloom, lean but strong, cruel eyes twinkling. One of them leered behind a wiry beard, black teeth grinding in anticipation of a kill. They were devils more than men, conditioned by a Captain crueller than any other.

Thesden swung his glaive high then brought it down fiercely on the first pirate. The Buccaneer reacted fast; he dodged to the side and brought up his buckler. Thesden's pole arm cleaved the small shield, splitting it in two. The pirate dropped it and held his cutlass with two hands. Thesden kicked the buckler aside and readied himself to strike again.

Raklen feinted a high strike, turned a full circle and then struck low with his sword. The pirate, totally fooled by the move, could only watch as Raklen's sword severed his leg. He cried out, blood spraying a nearby tree, which he used to steady himself. He then lashed out in response but his cutlass was easily deflected by Raklen's sword.

Satisfied that the first two pirates were distracted, Gam easily slipped around the battling men, his senses straining into the darkness and mist - seeking to move around behind the Wraith and his minions. The prospect was exciting and the adrenalin was pumping hard. All that Gam could hear now was the pounding of his own heartbeat and the rasping wheeze at the back of his throat as he drew breath into his burning lungs and enthused ever closer to his goal.

Raklen finished off his adversary and also strode onwards towards the Wraith's position in the mist.

Thesden swung his glaive again at the pirate; unfortunately he ducked and the glaive sliced into a lone tree where there it remained, stuck. Thesden attempted to free his glaive but the pirate, trying to take advantage of the situation, forced him to stop. Thesden punched out at the foul smelling individual with a gauntleted fist. The man staggered back, spitting blood. Before he could recover, Thesden pounced, brandishing two daggers. The pirate felt a searing heat across his neck as Thesden sliced it open; blood spurted from the open wound. In a vain attempt, the sea-dog tried to contain his lifeblood by clamping his hands about his neck, then blackness washed over him and he fell to the marshy ground. Thesden span his daggers, whirling them between his fingers before placing them back in his wrist sheathes. So intent was he on the kill he had not noticed the murderous eyes of the Wraith fixed so upon him, even with the mist. The Wraith turned to a beast of a man at his shoulder and pointed out the farmer-come-warrior. The pirate, dressed in red and black leathers and sporting a demonic mask similar in style to the Wraith's very own beaten-metal visage, nodded and hefting a large club menacingly stalked towards Thesden.

The Wraith flipped open an old leather-bound tome and sniggered maniacally, intoning, "lands to conquer in deaths dark vein, the slaughter of the sceptic, they shall wither in pain. Acolytes will dance, in the blood of the sacrificed, a crazed jig of madness, succumbed to my evil, ABSOLUTE!"

The Wraith directed a finger at one of his fallen pirates when shockingly the corpse stood up, jerked its head to face Raklen and attacked. The noble, horrified at the sight, withdrew a long, ornate dagger to use with his sword. Two slimy tentacles near exploded from the thing's eyes; others emerged, ripping through its flesh until about eight grotesque tentacles projected from the corpse's torso, rotten and mould ridden.

"Thy improbus tongue, sickle and tear, maim the righteous, render souls bare, imbue me thy might, decay with thy sight!" laughed the Wraith, as Loewen retired to stand along side her demented father and his two surviving brutish pirate bodyguards.

Raklen lunged at the tentacled monster. It dodged with unusual speed, wrapping a glutinous tentacle around Raklen's left arm and tugging violently, in an attempt to knock Raklen over. Fortunately, he had already anticipated this move and was in the process of counter attack. He slashed upward at the tentacle holding him, severing it. The slimy appendage fell to the floor, still wriggling like a worm. Now free, Raklen put his combat skills into action. He drove his dagger into the creature, following up with his sword. He turned a half circle, putting his back to the creature, letting the sword's momentum carry it into the beast. The creature roared in pain as it was skewered through its middle. Raklen paused to hear the satisfying sound as the monster slid off his sword and readied himself to strike a killing blow. He cut in again and again at the monster, sending chunks of tentacle and flesh flying. Eventually in the midst of the raining blood, the creature collapsed, dead – again. Raklen threw off his tricorn, revealing his long dark hair and sparkling emerald-green eyes. He expertly tossed his dagger high and transferred his sword to his left hand, then back to his right. He re-caught the dagger with flare.

"Now Wraith, YOU die!" he shouted, confidently striding towards the pirate Captain.

"I think not, yo-ho-ho," the Wraith replied, snapping his fingers. Jendess and Krial, his last and trusted pirate bodyguards, charged towards Raklen, spitting curses and other profanities.

"Your evil power does not daunt me fiend!" said a voice stepping out of the mist from behind the Wraith. The self-professed pirate King jumped and turned to face the newcomer - and to his surprise he faced a portly fellow in stained robes, his face set as hard as rock.

Gam held his breath as he realised he had taken the Wraith by surprise - it could all be over in matter of moments if he just floored the devil. But if he had taken him by surprise why was he smiling from below his mask?

Gam reacted just as some notable edged weapon came streaking down toward him and had it had not been for the reflection in the Wraith's eyes that gave away the sword an instant before it swung, Gam would surely have perished under the blade. As it was though, he had spun away an instant before.

The Friar cursed and awkwardly spun again as a frenzy of sword swings came at him, this time the sword caught his robe and ripped it. In the brief time that Gam had to dodge the sword he analysed his options and positioned himself so he was no longer putting his back to the laughing Wraith and this new assailant, who had seemingly appeared from the very mist itself.

He caught a glance of the attacker's face. The figure was seemingly wrapped in the very darkness; all that the Friar could discern were piercing, crimson eyes staring from a face again lost in the blackness. Gam's face dropped and a sinking feeling of dread in the pit of his stomach made him swallow hard as he witnessed two extending canine teeth appear from the attackers grinning lips. A vampyre? Surely there was no such thing? The futility of the question was dismissed as he dodged the lightning attacks. Discovering how or why this thing existed would have to wait, should he survive the vicious assault. He had to think of a way to incapacitate the vampire, whose swings were getting closer and closer.

Gam's thought process was broken as he suddenly had to duck and dodge a series of calculating attacks. The cloak-wrapped figure was lightning fast in his combination attacks; those piercing, scarlet eyes sought any opening in Gam's blocks. It was only the Friar's experience in fighting minor undead that enabled him to fend off the speedy strikes.

Satisfied that he had successfully recovered from the surprise attack, he allowed himself to analytically think again… destroy the vampire and kill the Wraith who was left unengaged and close by.

During the last defensive combat, Gam had observed the Wraith stalk around him, attempting to get behind. Obviously no longer satisfied to observe and let the apparently fortuitous encounter between priest and undead play out, but to involve himself directly. As Gam spun and countered another attack, he was certain he observed the Wraith risk a concerned and focused glance at the vampire. Yes, there was definitely something there worth investigating - was the Wraith controlling this blood-sucker or not?

The pirate bodyguard Krial, lunged at Raklen, his sword deflecting off the noble's dagger. Raklen swung his sword backhanded, letting it fly through the air at great speed. The frenzy of blades drove Krial back, he attempted to protect himself with his sword but it was knocked away by Raklen's own swift sword. This left Krial un-protected. Seizing the advantage, Raklen thrust his sword toward Krial. Raklen's prized sword skewered the warrior through the chest. Krial shrieked, comprehending his certain death. Raklen turned his back on Krial and quickly knelt, his sword still buried deep in the pirate's chest. Blood spurted from the wound, spraying Raklen's sword. The Mortlake noble stood up, bringing the sword up with him. Krial's rib cage splintered as the blade tore through his body from the up-slicing blade. Treating the rotten scoundrel with contempt, Raklen did not watch him fall to the ground but instead frantically searched for the remaining pirate Jendess – why had he not joined the fray? And then, he finally saw him…

Thesden swung his glaive having recovered it from the tree when suddenly, charging out from the thickening mist came a large black and red clad pirate, wielding a two-handed, spherical-headed club.

The former militiaman realised that this figure was probably some sort of pirate heavy. He wore a black and red shirt, similar coloured breeches and his face was concealed by a black, leather mask in the form of a leering demon – proclaiming him as some fanatical zealot of the Wraith.

The pirate cultist swung his mace toward Thesden in vicious and surprisingly swift swings. The farmer' glaive would be relatively useless against such a heavy and lethal weapon and instead he dropped to the ground. The pirate swung again and Thesden quickly rose and lifted his leg, blocking the zealot's forearm and disrupting his swing. He lashed out with his other leg, catching the pirate across the face with his foot. Buying himself valuable time Thesden scrabbled away lifting his glaive. The large pirate steadied himself from the blow, cursed, and reciprocated by swinging his huge club around in a circle, drawing momentum and bringing it down toward the farmer again. This time however, he didn't meet the farmer's blocking foot, but his glaive instead.

Thesden sighed in relief and shouted in triumph as he succeeded in lifting his glaive in time to parry the brute. He cut at the pirate, before the fell warrior had time to recover, and the club-wielding individual stumbled back as the glaive found the pirate's face and succeeded in severing the demon mask and slashing his features. The pirate hollered in pain and fell away wiping the blood from his eyes. Thesden jumped to his feet and pursued the pirate thug as he back-peddled, clearing his face of blood. The pirate sensed that Thesden was approaching and though still half-blinded by his own blood, swung his lethal club to and fro in a hope to batter the farmer. Thesden easily countered the move by sidestepping and dodging until he stalked to attain a position where the pirate's wild swings were not quite reaching. Just as he lifted his glaive for an executing thrust, a nearby pirate - who had been coolly observing the battle - shouted a warning to the fanatic who thusly corrected his stance and swung his club where it nearly slammed into the farmer.

"Hell has emptied and all the devils roam here!" shouted Danick spinning from the outskirts of a nearby combat with a group of ratmen and hacked down the pirate who had broken away from the main group to shout the warning. The pirate gurgled something indiscernible and slumped down. The Norseman disappeared as suddenly as he had arrived, back into the swirling maelstrom of flashing blades that was the main battle.

The Wraith's fanatic at last succeeded in wiping the stinging blood from his eyes, now that his guide had been slayed. He tried to focus on the farmer. Thesden ducked under the swings and spied his chance.

"Wraith, Wraith, imbue me thy might, Wraith, Wraith, slay with thy sight..." shouted the pirate, as he involuntarily stepped forward following after the heavy swinging club. Thesden ducked again and came up within the fanatic's outstretched arms. The glaive was too large a weapon to swing at this range, so instead Thesden just lifted it's point toward the pirate's neck, finding his throat. The Wraith's champion blurted a curse of surprise as the glaive tore into his throat and up through the back of his neck. Thesden held his weapon there a little longer as his enemy's blood began to pump from the fatal wound and he circled the shuddering pirate, gripping the glaive so that the dying man had no choice but to follow his move. The zealot dropped his large club and his eyes rolled up. Thesden withdrew his glaive and the Wraith's henchman slumped down to the ground in an ever-increasing pool of blood.

Suddenly a blade cut at Thesden, punching through his body. He screamed as his broken body fell away, his once bright blue cloak fell in tatters, showered with his blood. He fell to his knees in shock and now deafened to the noise of the battle around him.

"Let your enemies go before you my son. You have learnt everything I can teach you... you are ready. Go now, make me proud..." Thesden exhaled as he fell to the Barrowdale soil, the voice of his father carrying the last words he had said to him, before he had left to live in the Dale. "...I *am* proud."

Thesden spent his last breath whispering a prayer.

Raklen shouted in anger as he at last charged into the murdering Jendess and engaged him in combat. Over the clamour of the battle Thesden had not heeded the noble's warning call.

Gam's eyes welled up as he saw his friend Thesden cut down by Jendess. He doubled his effort, letting the farmer's determination inspire him against the vampire. He gripped his hammer and charged at the creature again, "for Barrowdale!"

The Wraith smiled as he foresaw victory emerging; he started chanting some sort of a ritual at the only remaining threat and paused just long enough to curse, "that damned Mortlake is at last going to suffer my wrath!"

The Wraith sought the last line of the Convene Deceased with his grubby finger and chanted the script of blood scrawl from his thick book in a low, guttural tongue. In turn, it glowed faintly, enhancing the menacing deep shadows of his mask and sparkled in his deep, malevolent eyes. He looked to his daughter and gently went to caress her face as she beamed up at him. At the last moment, his hand turned and he backhanded her across the face. Loewen gasped and crumpled to the soggy meadow.

"I could have achieved so much more with that statue of yours had you not so foolishly lost it!" he spat down at his daughter, his rage barely controlled.

"Still..." he trailed off, re-focusing on the battle. "Drawn to the desolate darkness, as a moth to a zealous flame, abused, butchered and defiled my child, animated unlife - there is no pain... come, let me further our exalted, hellish aim!" he chanted the final sentence and scintillating energy bolts leapt from the pages and disappeared high into the night sky. In response a lightning bolt crackled above and the bright light given off blinded all those who stared. The Wraith shouted with triumph as the corpses of the dead pirates strewn around him began to twitch and stir. They sat up and then slowly, in an unsettling, juddery motion, stood - their gaping mouths crying to the heavens, each one of them eager to kill and feast on the living. And apart from being thoroughly evil, they all had one similarity; they were all under the Wraith's control.

Raklen gasped as the Wraith, pirate King and black-magic practitioner, sent a wave of the undead pirates to attack the Chandorian militia and bolster their living kin.

The sadistic pirate King jumped in the air, hopping from foot to foot. The power he had, the raw evil energy. His eyes bulged as he watched his minions go to work.

A half dozen zombies snatched at a militiaman who was running for his life away from the spawn of evil. They caught the man and over the sound of his terrified screams and blood curdling moans, ripped him to pieces, showering the Barrowdale earth in his blood. Carnage and destruction had returned to this ancient land. Bedlam reigned supreme and a chaos that the land had not witnessed for several thousand winters was revisited.

The zombies began to lick up and devour what was left of the Chandorian soldier, some of the foul creatures began to rip into another, throwing up body parts as in jubilation.

"Arcane words, uttered over departed interred, commune the locution, animate the dead, raise the defunct, the rites have been read! You lose, little people," smirked the Wraith. "YOU LOSE!" The depraved pirate Captain cackled loudly, "Yo-ho-ho, my wonderful sea-dogs, slice 'em and dice 'em! Now KILL the noble Mortlake, kill him. All you zombies, KILL HIM!" He then looked to Gam, "let your God help you now!"

The Wraith's insane laughter rang across the Barrowdale sky like a wave, hell bent on slaughter!

CHAPTER EIGHT

30th and last night,

Lunar Cycle of the Cursed Constellation, 1189 Winters.

Satisfied that his zombies would soon slay the Chandorian Militia and Raklen Mortlake, the Wraith turned to Gam – eager to finish him off quickly. The Pirate reached for a dagger and launched it at the Friar with the best of his ability.

"Ye should have stuck to pirating! But then, ye don't even have a feckin' ship, I can't even see a piddling row-boat!" exclaimed Gam, briefly turning to face the Wraith, allowing himself to tear his eyes away from the vampire. Gam dodged one last time from the swiftly swinging sword, ducking under the vampire's lunge and rising to meet the pirate's spinning blade through the air, head on. He plucked it from the air with his hand, half spinning from the momentum and span directly back, releasing the Wraith's dagger back at him, before dodging another sword descent. That all happened in an instant, and as Gam came out of his dodge - positioning himself with the vampire behind and the Wraith in front - he was able to witness the surprised expression on the pirate's face as his own blade went spinning into his shoulder. Gam concealed his own surprise.

Sensing that the vampire was right behind him and vaguely surprised that the dagger's flight had been true, he sprinted as fast as his bulk would allow him at the Wraith. Gam swiftly shrugged off his over-robe and tossed it toward the pirate – it was the only thing that occurred to him. The robe enveloped the Wraith and left him sprawling back, still reeling from the shock of both his wound and the deft move from a fat and relatively insignificant friar. The superior sentiment he had been feeling up to now left in a wave of dizzying nausea and his sudden worry soon began to turn into blind panick. Loewen was still on the ground and only now began to stir from her father's clout.

Satisfied that the move had incapacitated the Wraith for a moment, Gam sprung, kicking out at the closing vampire from behind. Surprisingly his feet impacted with the vampire's face, catching him under the chin and knocking him away. The action was difficult to pull off and he lost his balance in the process, however it gained him valuable time. An icy chill clenched his foot from the impact with the undead creature. The pain and numbness were intense but he pushed the feeling aside, he certainly didn't have time to worry about that now.

Meanwhile, the snarling of the undead pirates rose into the night like the devil's chorus. They jumped on Militiamen, pinning and killing them - ripping the soldiers with plague-ridden fingernails and sharp, brutal teeth. The zombies were more advanced than their slow moving and dim-witted cousins. They were quick and efficient hunters - deadly to engage as they seemed to retain a level of animal instinct. The Chandorian warriors cried out, regrouped - back to back - ready to die for each other and in the service of their home.

Gam got to his feet, rising right up and under the Wraith's wild swings just as the self-professed pirate King managed to shrug off the robe. Having no time in which to draw his cutlass, he just managed to lift a second dagger up to meet the Friar's hammer now coming to bear on him. The Wraith could do little to fend off the powerful hammer strike with such a small weapon. The first strike sent the dagger flying from his grip as it caught it squarely on the pommel and he recoiled his hand in pain. The second strike caught him a glancing hit as he recoiled, knocking him away and down to the ground to join his wicked daughter.

Gam could not allow giving the pirate an inch, if he did relent - even for a brief moment - then the Wraith would be on him with his lethal cutlass, but, he also knew that the vampire would have surely recovered by now and continued his pursuit. He was correct.

Gam turned from the sprawling Wraith, just in time to meet a rapidly descending sword. With his hammer held high it met the sword just above the pommel and Gam was able to stop the potent attack. However, the vampire compensated and tugged sharply on it's sword. The blade caught the hammer shaft in its backward sweep, ripping it from the Friar's grip and it landed a five pace away. Surprised but unflinching, Gam reciprocated by sweeping his braced arm low and hard, causing the vampire to dodge back.

Reprieved for a brief moment and furiously focused, Gam turned back to the recovering Wraith and shoved him back to the ground again - right into a recovering Loewen - reclaiming his hammer in the same instance and turning immediately to counter the swift vampire yet again.

Gam surprised himself with the ferocity of his counter attack and even succeeded in knocking back the vampire. Hoping to take advantage of the situation, he drove at the sword again, pushing it further away and opening the vampire's block. Instinctively, Gam struck with his hammer again and gasped with relief as the hammer found the vampire's face and pulverized it. The warrior instinct of his early life had kicked in sometime ago - the training working him into lethal gear. The vampire fell away with a cry, it's face grotesquely caved in. Gam faltered as he was about to strike again as the vampire blurted something that caught his attention. Even though the being was trying to talk through broken teeth, he managed to catch the word *control*.

"What?" asked Gam, preparing to strike – knowing only too well that the vampire would regenerate from the wound shortly. "What did ye say, speak now or never!"

"I..I haven't much time, the control is weak because of the W..Wraith's wound – he has control over m..me..." the Vampire grunted as his face began to rebuild itself thanks to the supernatural regenerating powers of a child of the night. "Q..Quick - In life I w..was a Master Savant and I was the Wraith's c..conspirator and a practitioner of his demonology lore, until he realised I was of better use to him in this new guise you see before you n..now..."

Gam hesitated, his mind flashed back to Bethe's diary and her brother's tale – this sounded all too familiar. "You're Ritic Vilan?" Gam blurted and blinked away the surprise as the vampire began to snap out of it's pained trance and re-focus on him with cold, crimson eyes. Gam released with his hammer and continued to do so before the vampire could regenerate. He struck countless times, amid exploding blood and gore. Gam thrust his hand into his pack and emerged with a wooden stake, muttering gratitude to Gutiso's store. He aimed it over the vampire's chest and struck down hard with his hammer. The vampire screamed an unholy wail as it clawed at the stake sticking out of it's chest. Blood erupted from the wound in a spiralling pillar, showering Gam who fell back with shock at the gruesome event. The vampire flailed about, kicking and snatching at the air – Gam dived back in and maintained his grip on the stake, driving it all the way through. He could hear a horrific tearing noise as the vampire tensed and exploded, showering the area with quick-rotting gore and guts.

A very blood-soaked friar turned to a recovering Wraith and smiled wickedly - with even greater effect due to so much dripping redness. Gam had an idea. Was this vampire - whilst momentarily free of the Wraith's mental control - trying to tell him something specific? After all, Gam had Cordale's dark little secret in his very pack – the evil, skin-bound book which originally belonged to Ritic Vilan, the confidant of the Wraith.

A burly, barrel-chested individual, Jendess's coarse, blunt features were balanced by cauliflower ears. His reputation was murky to say the least, and, according to most, bordered on the vicious. He used his sword like a cleaver and Raklen spun, dodged and side-stepped the great oafish swings. It was Jendess's turn to dodge as Raklen struck back and nicked the burley man's face with his fast blade, drawing blood. Before the pirate lieutenant could even curse, Raklen had weaved inside the warrior's guard surprising him. There was no way he could respond and Raklen brought down his sword in a great arc. The weapon cut into the pirate's shoulder and sliced down almost to his stomach. Raklen withdrew his sword and then stabbed through Jendess's middle. The noble drew close to the pirate's face, "my sword seeks your heart for repayment of a life taken, a Dalesman's life, Thesden's life - his was worth a thousand of yours. Scum." He floored the big warrior with derision and hurriedly glanced around scanning the battlefield.

Danick with the Chandorian Militia were half their original number and it was clear to see that they would all soon perish under the zombie's brutal assault. The remaining Wraith pirates fell back, leaving the hard work to their undead kin and then at last spied the three heroic companions behind and the assault on their captain.

Raklen nodded his head to them in mock respect as they launched a screaming charge toward Gam in order to protect the Wraith. Raklen intercepted the group before they could reach the Friar and span his rapier style sword and long-bladed dagger with murderous grace toward the weapon-wielding pirates, awaiting the onslaught.

Raklen span and ducked under one thrust, slashing the first snarling pirate across the waist and spilling his opponent's guts across the ground. He came up under his duck, countered one black blade, parried another, and repost with his own, thrusting his weapon into the heart of another.

After dodging a pirate that attacked him from behind, Raklen ducked and weaved, parried again and brought his dagger across the exposed neck of the pirate. The evil buccaneer clamped his hands around his neck, trying to contain his life blood, until Raklen ran him through with his sword and turned the unfortunate fell warrior – who then received a further two stabs from his fellows as they rushed in from another angle. The two pirates cursed in alarm, thinking they had killed their kin and whirled in anger on Raklen. But the young Mortlake had predicted their response and soared at them, his own blades whirling in a half-circle that cut down the pirates in their tracks.

That was half of their number and the noble hadn't even broken stride as he advanced through the enemy, protecting Gam's flank.

Raklen span again and hurled his ornate dagger at a fast approaching and screaming pirate - sending him to his knees - and then Raklen ignored him while he parried, countered and thrust at another of his attackers, running him through with his blade. Sensing the pirate's positions around him as they countered with their own thrusts, he dextrously dived over one wild, lashing blade and parried another, landing next to the kneeling and dying pirate. He rescued his dagger, slashing the pirate's throat as he did so for good measure and whirled around to counter another biting sword seeking his heart. He did so with ease and sent it's wielder crashing to the ground – a bloody criss-cross marking the pirate's chest. Recovering from his whirlwind move he brought his dagger and sword together, skewing another unfortunate pirate through the seaman's head. The evil fighter dropped his sword as he went into violent spasms and Raklen withdrew his blades and kicked the body away. It was then that Raklen noticed a pirate loom up to Gam's exposed back, he went to call out, terrified of the prospect of losing another comrade in such a way, when an axe came sweeping down from behind the assailant nearly cleaving the pirate in two.

"Keep fighting. Keep fighting!" shouted Bane, wrenching his axe free, "those bloody zombies will be on us in a heartbeat!"

Raklen flashed the dwarf a grateful smile and nodded, hastily moving back to Gam's other side.

"That's the second time ye've saved mi life!" exclaimed Gam over the clang of steel.

" And to think you were going to leave me behind!" replied Bane, hacking down a pirate. "Now the way your staring at that thrice-damned book, I be guessing ye can use it - so use it all ready!" he urgently called. "You can use the book surely - you *are* a bloody priest!"

Gam suddenly looked like a man stuck between the proverbial rock and a hard place but started to scan through the skin-bound, occultist's book nonetheless.

A small group of the Chandorian militia were working together and succeeded in cutting down one of the pirate zombies, showing great courage in seeking to shine in front of a Mortlake. Unfortunately, this was not the time for foolhardy heroics and they did not stand a chance against these creatures that walked beyond death. A cluster of the devilish monsters pounced at the young men, teeth chattering hysterically in eager anticipation of the kill. Tasting the fear in the air and thriving on it, they struck. A zombie landed on one militiaman driving the unfortunate soldier hard into the ground, snapping bones. A brief cry of surprise and then pain blurted from the warrior as he died from the extreme brutality of the undead assault and thrashed in the throws of death. No sooner had the first man been floored, the second foul creature struck with terrific speed to rake it's clawed hands at another of the warriors and subsequently hurled the shocked man into another of his fellows - sending them both reeling into a broken heap on the battlefield. The Chandorian warriors had not managed to land a single blow before they were decimated.

Anger rose like rolling flame within Raklen Mortlake as he observed the vile encounter and was unable to do a thing about it at the moment.

'Their sacrifice will not be in vain!' he vowed, spinning his sword and dagger in defiance and directly into a zombie, as he and Bane desperately worked to defend Gam from the pirate zombies – whilst the Friar looked to counter the Wraith's foul work.

Bane kicked out, his foot making contact with a zombie's knee. The crack was quite audible and the creature sprawled backwards. Simultaneously and with the agility of a cat, Bane ducked back from another zombie but found the space and time to release two daggers toward the first and now kneeling zombie, which was at the dwarf's height. By the time he was steady on his feet from the dodge, both daggers were buried up to the hilts in the zombie's eyes. The undead pirate roared and attempted to violently shake it's head to clear the objects from it's eye sockets. It began to whine in frustration, resorting to sniffing the dwarf out. Benefiting from the creature's blindness, Bane sprang, axe raised and cocked to strike. The zombie somehow sensed his movements but could do nothing as the dwarf's axe cut down it's back, slicing through muscle and bone alike, until it sliced all the way through. Now two parts, the zombie fell to the ground pumping out foul smelling blood. Bane shook the blood off his axe and spat at the cleft corpse, turning to face the next grotesque. He countered a zombie's deadly hand with his axe's shaft and brought it down hard, half wrenching, half slicing, the creature's arm off. Without breaking step and with the zombie thusly unable to defend it's midriff he hacked into it's stomach until it dropped. Before he could even breath hard another zombie pounced and he just managed to block it's strikes, knowing that should he falter, either Gam or

Raklen would be exposed to attack. As long as they worked together and protected each others flanks and backs, they would survive.

Though Bane countered this latest assault as best as he could, in his near exhausted state he could not keep up the fight to stop all the zombie's strikes. The creature sensed the dwarf's slowing parries and launched a flurry of cold, calculating attacks against him - only a few of which were blocked by the old dwarf.

Bane shouted a warning to his two comrades, temporarily fending off the zombie pirates; it didn't last. Bane fell back, his axe falling from his hand. He saved himself with his arms, only for them to be kicked out by one of the demented zombies, sending him down to the cold, wet ground. Bane's mind filled with the cold realisation that his time had come. His comrades couldn't help him now; he was on his own.

A zombie began to kick him repeatedly with absurd strength, another stamped on his head, determined to keep the dwarf down and dead. Bane began to rise. He fumbled for his last dagger and in desperation, buried it deep into the kicking zombie's leg. It may as well have been a toothpick for the good it did. The crazed, cold determination of the undead was shocking, as Bane once again fell with a barrage of kicks. Out of the corner of his bloodied eye, Bane caught sight of Raklen's shocked face and he read the helplessness in those human and caring eyes, as the noble desperately fought the zombies, frantically trying to reach and help him.

The Mortlake's actions almost fell into a slow motion as the dwarf's head violently jerked and swayed from the pummelling feet. Soon darkness began to blur Bane's vision, until he was blinded by the onslaught and his strength left him. The zombies crowded around his sprawled form and white, rheumy eyes focused on a Friar's exposed back.

The Wraith looked perturbed as he faced off against Gam. Both of them clutched large, bound tomes, no further than a good ten paces from each other. The Wraith flicked open his book, attempting to raise more of his wretched pirates. He looked to Gam and noticed a confidence in the Friar's eyes that hadn't been there a short while ago. Gam held the book aloft, his finger marking a certain page.

"Your time has come pirate, your undead minions can't help ye now! I'll see you dead in a five-breath or see you hanged in Cheth at Lord Mortlake's convenience - which'll it be?" questioned Gam.

"I call that bold talk for a drunken fat man!" replied the Wraith, smirking. Gam looked livid and bellowed conclusively, "dig your grave, you son-of-a-bitch!"

The Wraith took his cue and launched into a demonic chant, the guttural words pouring from his mouth and making all those of stout heart and in ear- shot grimace from the pain pounding in their ears.

"Thy improbus tongue, sickle and tear, maim the righteous, render souls bare, imbue me thy might, decay with thy sight..."

Gam shook his head, looking peeved, "Yeah, I heard that one before. Ye truly are a nut!" Gam read assuredly from Ritic Vilan's book, a chant that would cancel the Wraith's nefarious necromantic and imbuing power, "once foretold on life, the world is fraught with evil strife, the kind that comes to seal your fate, escape your wrong doings, 'fore it's too late!" Gam raised his hand theatrically and pointed at a stunned Wraith. The pirate King held his breath, suddenly recognising the book wrapped in the Friar's arms. He fearfully observed the zombies assailing the Chandorians. The uneasiness was replaced with a smug smile as nothing seemed to happen, but then, suddenly, a zombie began to falter, allowing the militiamen to hack it down. A cheer rose up as more of the zombies began to fall to their knees and discordant wails lifted to the sky as they finally collapsed to the ground. The Chandorian militia spurred forward into the last few pirates who, up until now had been happy to let the zombies do all the work.

The Wraith's irate screams joined with his fading zombie's in a sickening cacophony until he levelled profanities at Gam and slammed shut his wicked tome. The zombies which were gaining the upper hand against Raklen and crowding around to get at Gam fell in an awkward and sickening tangle to the ground - helped on their way by the noble's sword. The ones responsible for assailing Bane also fell and Gam was relieved to see that the dwarf's chest still rose and fell.

The Wraith withdrew his long curved sword and charged at Gam. The Friar was about to meet the charge when Raklen stepped up to his side, "leave him to me Gam – let me put this affair right once and for all."

Gam nodded and spied Loewen creeping around behind Danick as he fought the remaining pirates, her darting eyes betraying her murderous intention. She pounced, little fingers extended and long nails seeking the soft flesh around the wilderness warrior's throat and eyes. She ripped at his face as he cried out, her nails wielded like stiletto blades – plunging in and out. Blood released from his neck as if by a carrion-feeding beak. It was brutal, demonic, sick.

The abuse at the hands of her father and the poisonous statue that she had wielded had taken their toll.

Gam spurred into motion after the juvenile assassin, hammer cocked and under his full control, "what fell and foul insanity shrouds your young brow?" intoned Gam as she cackled coldly – her evil triumphant act realised and suddenly met with a face-full of cold steel, knocking her unconscious.

Raklen leaped up, bringing his sword arcing down toward the Wraith. The strike was parried by the pirate King but it still caught his arm and showered him with blood. The Wraith snarled and backed off a little in surprise.

"Your skill has improved little Mortlake, but no matter, I shall finish you and then your petty family will follow after you – six feet under, by my hand!"

Raklen steeled his nerve and spun his sword and dagger in anticipation. He swung his sword, bringing it down fiercely; unfortunately the Wraith was expecting the strike and clearly held a greater skill in swordsmanship. He countered Raklen's sword and then struck out with a wicked, curved dagger in his left hand. Raklen instinctively leapt back to avoid the blade but it scratched across his chest, drawing blood. The noble did not allow himself to be distracted by the wound and instead let his sword spin from the deflection and carry in a circle around his head to bring it back around and down at the Wraith. Again, his sword was deflected. Raklen took a half step back to re-calculate his next move and regard the pirate's stance to hopefully detect his next assault. He could see the Wraith's beady eyes through the vision slits in his ghostly mask which added an element of maniacal evil. The Wraith sensed Raklen's apprehension and laughed, hard.

"If you think you are going to strike me down and leave with your life, you are sorely mistaken."

Raklen countered, holding his sword out in challenge. The Wraith tilted his head like an adult might to a babe and mocked the noble.

"Fine!" commented Raklen, "have it your way!" He wielded his sword as easily as a stick, striking the Wraith's sword to the side and punching him in the face. He turned suddenly, bringing his sword around to strike the dagger from the Wraith's grip. His sword succeeded in finding the pirate's hand, cutting it harshly and the Wraith dropped his dagger.

Raklen spun again, avoiding the Wraith's counterstrike but had to spin a second time, rather than committing to another strike as the Wraith's sword came careering down at him again. Instead, the noble landed a kick on the pirate, knocking the cursing devil back into a gorse bush.

Raklen, breathing heavily, began to realise that he would be hard-pressed to defeat the Wraith's skill with a sword. His best chance was to end it quickly – the longer the fight continued the more likely the Wraith would win. Raklen continued after him - and barely dodging another swing - brought the pommel of his sword around into the Wraith's face, buying himself some time. With a frenzy of blows Raklen succeeded in cutting the pirate King and followed up with a hard uppercut, catching the bloodied Wraith under his chin. Raklen let himself a sigh of relief as the Wraith dropped to one knee, but as soon as he had, he was up bringing his sword around sharply. It was a rouse; Raklen realised and just managed to bring his sword up in time to parry the strike. The two blades met with a clang of steel and Raklen had to take another step back.

All of a sudden, whispers came to the fighting pair; they carried on the sea wind and intertwined with the very mist surrounding them. The Wraith looked this way and that, trying to make out the source of the voices. He shook his head violently, trying to stem the voices invading his mind.

"No! Your Dale belongs to me! You can't have it back!" he shouted to the very mist encircling him. Raklen looked on in shock and thought he could make out ghostly faces appearing in the fog but they disappeared as soon as he focused on them, to reappear somewhere else, and where as the voices were mere whispers to the noble, apparently to the Wraith they were piercing screams. He heard whisperings of fell warnings against the pirate King and realised they were the spirits of true Dalesmen and the love of the dale stayed with them even in death. They would not have it perverted and ruined by the likes of this black-hearted killer and Raklen agreed ten-fold. He had heard many a fearful folk chit-chatting of the Sea Spectres haunting Barrowdale but they had it wrong - they were not all maniacal spirit hosts, they were compassionate Dale folk.

"I follow this path with controllable wrath, hunting a disciple of curse. You magician of evil, conjurer of corruption, killer, pirate and worse!" Stepping up to the distracted Wraith, Raklen ran him through with his blade. The pirate's eyes shot open and he coughed blood, "this is not how it was supposed to b..be..."

Raklen withdrew his blade and let the self-professed pirate King of Barrowdale fall to the ground. Their job complete, the spirits in the mist withdrew and vanished.

"What did ye utter?" asked Gam stepping up to the noble's side as Raklen breathlessly whispered a string of words and stood over the Wraith's corpse. The noble looked to the Friar and surveyed the surviving Chandorians as they drew around the two men. Each man breathed heavily, leaning on swords - more use as walking sticks than weapons now. He repeated his words in stronger measure, "the sound of water running off a fall, the wind through time-gnarled willow trees. A glade of bluebells. Ferns reclaiming an old ruin, a bubbling brook by a peaceful hamlet. The morning bird call, the village pond, a tree-house on the outskirts of a farm, a lazy summer morning where butterflies kiss the blooms," he looked to the faces of the men drawn around him, "I love all such things... of Barrowdale, and I will see them stay."

The Chandorians looked to Raklen Mortlake and stood just a little taller. Gam nodded his agreement to Raklen - truly a sworn protector of Barrowdale and a worthy future lord.

***

As the Chandorian militia began to recover the bodies of the fallen, a young corporal with heavy stubble and blood stains to his face beckoned Gam over as they clamped Loewen in irons.

"Out of the black my zombie did call..." began Loewen. Gam stared at her sunken and cruel face, there was almost nothing left of that once pretty and innocent face.

"What?" Gam asked, holding back the Chandorian guard's arm, "I believe she's trying to tell me something."

"My pain and suffering it conveyed to you all..." she mumbled, staring passed him and at nothing in particular.

Gam then realised that she was reciting some rhyme, but more to herself than him. She was past all sense and sanity and now her features looked quite simple in the bright moon light.

"The Chandorian children would cry under beds..."

The Friar realised that the statue, coupled with her father's treachery had driven her completely insane.

"...for the fear that my zombie would bite off their heads," she chuckled maniacally.

"Poor child," intoned Gam, shaking his head. He glanced at the guard with sad eyes. "Take her away."

Suddenly Loewen yelled and her face twisted into a contorted visage of pain. The sudden outburst made Gam and Raklen jump and wheel around to face her, only to see the Wraith - not quite taken by death - thrust his dagger into his daughter's back. Gam reacted without thinking and brought his hammer down on the Wraith's skull. Messy and crude but it took the Wraith into the afterlife just the same.

"O my god, I'm dying, help me!" Loewen cried, looking to Gam with coherent eyes once more. Gam dropped to his knees and lifted her head, cradling her tiny body. "Help me Gam, please!" she pleaded, fighting the pain.

"I can't do a thing for ye girl. Your father's killed ye and I've done for him."

"Don't leave me laying here Gam, don't let the wolves get me." she uttered from dry and cracking lips. Gam nodded, "I'll see that ye get buried."

"I'll see you again Gam," Loewen managed to utter. "Walking the streets of g..glory."

"Don't count on it child," he whispered, but she was already gone.

EPILOGUE

1st Noon, Lunar Cycle of the Dragon's Heart Constellation,
1189 Winters.

Gam flexed his toes and rubbed in between his pinkies soothingly. He let out a sigh. The bath water was delightfully hot and he took to rubbing his legs gingerly. He had bruises on top of bruises. But at least now, lying in this hot water, complete with scented oils, all his aches and pains had departed. It was joyful. He sighed again, louder. He would have to keep the seedy but friendly Betsy's Bath House a well deserved little secret – especially the girly, scented oils part.

"That's a big sigh," said a voice to his left. "Feels good doesn't it?"

Gam glanced to his immediate left through the rising steam to observe Raklen, sat in a tin tub exactly like the Friars'. Gam smiled, 'a secret to all except Raklen!'

The noble's face was covered in a soapy foam and with a worn mirror balanced on his knees he was shaving very carefully with a small, sharp dagger.

A splash to Gam's other side attracted his eyes – head unmoving – to his right, where there, sat in a similar tub, was Bane.

'Alright, well a secret to all except Raklen *and* Bane!' Gam let himself a chuckle.

The dwarf had his long, copper-coloured hair tied up over his head, fixed in place with his long beard and trailing moustache – it was quite a bizarre sight and the ties looked almost like little bows. Bane seemed unfazed and quite happy unlike his usual grumpy sodness. In fact, by his appearance, Gam guessed that a dwarf who had already celebrated his four hundredth birthday was unconcerned with appearances - he didn't do handsome for handsome's sake.

A line of bath tubs stretched off to each side of Raklen and Bane, each had a little table sporting a marvelous little mosaic picture. Upon the tables sat a selection of bath oils, brushes, small cleaning cloths and a platter of nibbles. Gam noted that Bane's oils remained unused but the selection of brushes were floating lazily around the dwarf.

Betsy's Bath House was empty bar the three of them, so goodness knows why they chose the tubs immediately next to his - they looked quite the peculiar trio. Cosy. Still, it had been an outstanding idea and after the somber and chilly morning, very much appreciated.

After sun-up the three of them had set off from Frostcross to the chapel. They had already received word that the Tralleign children had met up with their explorer father, Captain Tralleign, and were returning to Frostcross ahead of a contingent of Chandorian Militia to sweep the Meddle. With the dispatch rider that had brought the news, also came three notes. Each was folded in half, sealed privately with wax with the Mortlake family coat-of-arms pressed into it.

As the coastal wind had gently buffeted the companions, they had paid their respects to the cluster of new simple markers indicating the graves of Thesden, Danick, Mayam, Jonah's remains and the other citizens of Barrowdale who had lost their lives in the Wraith's attack on their beloved dale. But soon, stood as they were on the exposed grassy hill overlooking Frostcross, a strong wind had begun, blowing in from the sea. The rough fray crashed into the rocks far below, adjacent to the Twilight Maidens. Gam had briefly stopped at an un-marked and new gravestone on the far side of the chapel, quite out of the way and next to a small embankment.

Gam had simply scratched an 'L' near the base of the stone and whispered a quick prayer. They then returned to Frostcross as the strong squall had began to cause the eerie, howl of the ocean, or known as it's local name; Dead Man's Scream.

A stiff breeze suddenly knifed down Gam's neck, reminding him of the earlier chill and he shuddered, hunkering down to his lowest chin in the aromatic hotness of the tub.

"How do you think Jonah knew about the statue and the secret passage to the coast?" asked Raklen carefully shaving his cheek with the knife.

"I believe he discovered the passage by accident, just as I," replied Gam, closing his eyes to unwind. "I've been thinkin' about this for sometime. I reckon he settled in Frostcross and took to a spot of tomb robbin' after learning the tales of the statue from a pirate raid here many winters before. I remember Bardon himself telling the story in the Fool's Nook of a raid where a young Jonah was allowed to escape with his Master's body. He had visited Barrowdale as a boy and the events of that raid had stayed fixed in his young mind and flourished. I remember uncoverin' various rumours in differing texts, held in the Tinhallow library, which told of an ancient secret lost under the Oakstone - some sort a ancient relic from a fallen empire."

Bane murmured an agreement, "some things just cannot be explained and the origins of this cursed statue, I guess, in this adventure, is one of them. Something evil from the dawn of the world and it falls to us few to never reveal its location." Bane turned to Gam and Raklen, "to never reveal the location of the statue and the Wraith's accursed tomes, do ye all swear it?" And there, in their bath tubs did they so swear it.

"One thing that I just don't understand," added Raklen, "is why did he even bother to leave a map with its location?"

"I think he wanted to do the right thing in the end and not let wickedness - like his former nefarious Captain - get hold of a considerable evil power," replied Bane. "I believe he had cause to give *me* the map. Before his life was cut short, Bardon had mentioned that old Jonah had been asking after me."

Gam nodded and searching the soapy faces of his new found friends and in turn, defenders of Barrowdale, uttered, "Jonah just wanted to do one good thing before the end of his days-" Gam paused in thought. The truth in the Friar's words resonated deep within each of the companions and sitting there, each one, including Gam, recognised within, their own individual and sometime shady past. Perhaps this was just the event they had needed in order to amend things. Gam continued, "-to be in the light, just for once, and not in the darkness."

Reflecting on their own past the companions glanced to each other in mute understanding.

"Curse the Wraith – glad he's dead and buried!" abruptly exclaimed Raklen. "Perhaps we should have stuck his head on a pike at the Shoremeet to ward off other pirates?"

Bane'e eyes shone, "Aye, boil down the head to a skull and inlay with silver and gems…" he trailed off to a whisper when noticing Gam's expression whilst reaching for the nibbles – realising that perhaps now wasn't the time.

The Friar lifted the platter of earthy, fat-lathered, arterial-clogging, porky Sweetmeats. He inhaled over the platter but smelt nothing. Raklen turned his nose up, face wrinkling – it was pointless sludge to him. The young noble instead plunged his fingers into a bowl, mincing around for the chopped pieces of translucent fish that glimmered freshly within. 'Very regional,' it occurred to him. Authentic, rustic - he winked at Gam - and unbelievably winning. He placed a morsel in his mouth, smiling as it coated his tongue.

Gam still looked a little uncomfortable and replaced his untouched platter of sweetmeats on the mermaid mosaic of the table. He glanced down to a small animal which scurried out of his voluminous hood - hanging on a rack by the tub - and onto his shoulder. Balthy's large brown eyes stared at the Friar as if to add further weight to Gam's guilt.

"O Blow it!" he exclaimed, sending a wave over the rim. The others looked up. "Look 'ere, all this niceness is making me think I should all tell yer the truth. I'm not a Friar right!"

"Not a Friar?" voiced Raklen and Bane as one.

"Aye, I'm a Sergeant in the Chandorian Militia. I was in charge of the Execution detail when the Wraith legged it!"

"When the Wraith escaped?" uttered Raklen, a deep frown creasing his brow.

"Aye. I was badly wounded in the break-out and, to my wife's dismay, I got ripped to the tits on booze and worse-"

Raklen raised his eyes at the Friar's decidedly ineloquent vocabulary. He was relieved that he wasn't a Cheth minister, yet, out here, he just seemed to fit in perfectly.

"-I was dismissed from the Militia and things went downhill from there - heck, we nearly lost our cottage! I was angry at everyone and everything, getting wankered at every opportunity, until one day I was approached by old Lord Mortlake, ye very own father," Gam indicated to Raklen, for possibly the benefit of Bane. "In private he helped me to realise I should be focusing and channelin' my rage against one individual. The one responsible for my rapid decent - the thrice-damned Wraith! Lord Mortlake gave me the opportunity to turn my life around. He sent me here, to Barrowdale, where uncanny supernatural happenings had been reported to him. I was to disguise myself as the new replacement friar in Frostcross. I was an Acolyte y'see, when I was plucked from the streets as a scruffy urchin but I chucked it in when I became disillusioned by the other Monks. Accordingly my background and knowledge had me set and in good standings for my new secret mission. Father Superior Dodge is a friend of Lord Mortlakes' and under his blessing did the mission go ahead and therefore he became the third and last person to know of my mission," Gam turned to Raklen. "He did not inform me that ye were in hiding here from the Wraith, he who had sworn revenge against ye so publicly for his imprisonment and sentenced execution." Gam indicated the open and discarded Mortlake note on the table.

"Likewise, my father failed to inform me of your true intentions and cover, Gam," added Raklen, shaking his head. "One assumes he was covering for the both of us. You would not be able to expose me as a Mortlake should anything befall you-"

Gam nodded and interrupted, "but ye would have an ally close at hand should ye need it. And I believe now, your father guessed that the Wraith was behind the blasted upsets here in Barrowdale and concerned that he was tracking ye down!"

"Clever fellow," added Bane, lighting his long pipe, drawing on the pipe with quick puffs and relaxing back into the tub.

"That's why he's a Lord!" replied Gam, chuckling and smirking like a toad. He gave Balthy a little stroke with his finger, "I must return ye to little Ysara when they return t'morrow eve as well, huh?" He turned back to his new friends, "Lord Mortlake gave me a purpose I so badly needed - to assist my kinsmen and redeem myself. I think mi wife was rather pleased!"

"Now I see why it was such a chore for you to combat the Wraith and his own blighted enchantments with Ritic Vilan's manual," chuckled Bane, remembering how he had pressed Gam into using it during the height of the battle.

Raklen hooted with laughter, imagining Gam struggling to read the enchantments. The noble had finished shaving and chortled, sploshed and gurgled through the water which he soothingly splashed onto his face.

Gam waited for the noble to finish laughing, "glad ye are amused at my expense. Well, think I'll get out before the water goes cold and any remaining self respect disappears completely! Look away both ye scoundrels!"

Bane removed the pipe from his lips long enough to utter, "come, come, its nothing that we haven't seen."

"I'd like to think ye haven't seen *me* master dwarf!" Gam chuckled.

Although they had only known each other for a relatively short time, they had gone through oodles together and already felt a good sense of deep friendship; a strong bond formed as brothers-in-arms.

Raklen, continuing to snigger but with his mind still dancing from Gam's disclosure suddenly burst out with, "that is why a contingent of Militia were on standby and secreted at Tinhallow with the monks!" he exclaimed in sudden realisation, beginning to stand from the tub also.

"But they must have already been on their way with the speed in which they had arrived at the Shoremeet to combat the Wraith - how did they know to come?"

Gam shook himself and fastened a thick cloth under his belly and negatively shrugged his shoulders to Raklen's question. Bane continued to merrily puff away on his pipe, eyes twinkling and with a smile playing about the corner of his mouth he announced cunningly, "Ah, well your father is a good friend of mine, see."

The young Mortlake suddenly stood bolt upright and the Chandorian Sergeant accidentally let his cloth fall to the ground at this sudden revelation. Standing as naked as shaved monkeys they stood in mute shock - this was a first for Gam.